"My little brothers think the world of you."

"I don't know when my heart has ever been won over to children so quickly. They're so sweet. So loving."

"A lot like you in that respect." He looked down at her, his expression tender.

Sensing his intentions, her heartbeat quickened in anticipation. But she couldn't let him kiss her, could she? Not until she discovered if Therese was wrong in her assumptions about his long-term level of devotion to the twins. To *her*.

As she well knew, the enticing feelings of "love" held little meaning if not built on a solid foundation of lasting commitment. But Sawyer had yet to speak of love. Shouldn't that fact alone put her on her guard?

Reluctantly she pressed her hand firmly to his chest and attempted to step back.

But he held her fast, his gaze intent. "Tori, I think you need to know that—"

With a reverberating clang the cowbell above the main door startled them apart.

"You were starting to say?" Tori encouraged.

He shrugged, avoiding her gaze. "Maybe it will come to me later."

Glynna Kaye treasures memories of growing up in small Midwestern towns—and vacations spent with the Texan side of the family. She traces her love of storytelling to the times a houseful of great-aunts and great-uncles gathered with her grandma to share candid, heartwarming, poignant and often humorous tales of their youth and young adulthood. Glynna now lives in Arizona, where she enjoys gardening, photography and the great outdoors.

The Nanny Bargain

Glynna Kaye

Recycling programs for this product may not exist in your area.

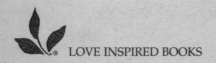

LOVE INSPIRED BOOKS

ISBN-13: 978-0-373-62276-4

The Nanny Bargain

Copyright © 2017 by Glynna Kaye Sirpless

www.Harlequin.com

Printed in U.S.A.

Let us draw near to God with a sincere heart
and with the full assurance that faith brings,
having our hearts sprinkled to
cleanse us from a guilty conscience.
—*Hebrews* 10:22

The Lord himself goes before you and will be
with you; He will never leave you nor forsake
you. Do not be afraid; do not be discouraged.
—*Deuteronomy* 31:8

To Maridor Keck, who loves God with all
her heart. Thank you for your friendship,
encouragement and prayers
as I continue on this writing journey.

Chapter One

"That's all there is to it," concluded Sawyer Banks from where he sat behind a weathered oak desk. He looked quite at home in the decidedly masculine-flavored office of his outdoor-gear shop, Echo Ridge Outpost. Leather. Wood. Wildlife prints on the knotty pine walls. "Piece of cake."

Easy for *him* to say. Victoria "Tori" Janner folded her hands primly in her lap, determined to hear him out. But if her best friend, Sunshine Carston, hadn't vouched for the rugged, blue-eyed outdoorsman, she wouldn't be sitting here one minute longer on this snowy February afternoon. What he'd outlined during this interview was troubling, at the very least.

"Apply for the childcare position," he recapped, his steady gaze holding hers, "and if you get it, I'll not only employ you here at the Outpost part-time, but behind the scenes I'll throw in an additional dollar an hour on top of whatever wage you agree on with the Selbys. Does that sound fair?"

More than fair. Suspiciously so.

Tori lifted her chin slightly, determined he wouldn't detect how uneasy his proposition made her feel. She needed the job—desperately—if she intended to remain in the mountain country community of Hunter Ridge, Arizona. Going "home" to life in Jerome was no longer an option if she could help it.

"If I'm understanding correctly, what your offer boils down to is if I get the childcare job, you want me to spy on the grandparents of your younger siblings and report back to you."

"Spy?" He shook his head with a laugh, his longish sun-streaked blond hair brushing the collar of his gray plaid shirt. Fine lines creased at the corners of his eyes. "That term's extreme for what I'm asking you to do— which is to provide a weekly update on activities and exercise, diet, moods and misbehaviors, and—"

"All that detail on the boys, or their grandparents, too?"

He stopped short, then laughed again. "I don't much care what Ray has for breakfast. Unless, of course, it negatively impacts Landon and Cubby in some way."

"Cubby?"

"Nickname for Jacob."

He made his proposition sound so benign. She felt silly challenging him and suspecting hidden motives. But she couldn't go into anything blindly, no matter how much she needed a job. "I'll be quite honest, Mr. Banks, I—"

"Honesty is exactly what I want. And discretion. Common sense." The corners of his mouth lifted. "And call me Sawyer."

She ignored his coaxing smile, one he'd undoubtedly perfected to sway female hearts. But she was newly immunized against that well-practiced male maneuver. "I require honesty, as well. Is it your intention for me to gather evidence that will enable you to take those children away from their grandparents? I don't want any part in that."

Her mom's mother had raised her, and she wouldn't accept a role that undermined the twins' relationship with their grandparents.

"Whoa." Sawyer held up his hands in defense, and she realized her brows had been lowered, her tone too sharp. Not how she wanted to come across to a potential employer. "Rest assured, Tori, that's not my intention. Far from it. I have no doubt Ray and Therese love the grandsons my dad fathered with their daughter. That's not the issue. The deal is that they've suddenly had to take on two active children. That's asking a lot of people who've reached the golden years of a retirement they've worked long and hard for. I'm just not convinced it isn't more than they can handle on their own."

He again sounded reasonable. Kind and caring. Why was she so distrustful? A residual effect of her ex-fiancé's abrupt departure, no doubt.

"While we're not close, I have a decent enough relationship with them and the boys." He turned in his chair to snag a photo off the bookshelf behind him and handed it to her. Gazing down at the towheaded, freckle-faced twins, she suspected the adorable twosome were the spitting image of Sawyer in his childhood.

"So I want to do whatever I can," he continued, "to ensure the welfare of kids and grandparents alike without it appearing that I'm meddling."

"Which is why…"

"Why I suggested they hire someone at least part-time to give them a hand. After months of debating the pros and cons between them, they're suddenly acting on it."

He raised a brow, awaiting her response.

Once more she glanced down at the photo, then placed

it on the desk. "How long, again, has it been since the fire?"

"Over a year. Fifteen months. The twins were almost three and a half years old at the time. Four and a half now. They'll start kindergarten in the fall."

"Heartbreaking." How well she knew life could be sailing along fine one minute and upended the next. "I'm sorry, too, that you lost your father and your—"

"Dad's wife. She was never my stepmother. They'd been married less than five years before…" A shadow seemed to pass over his features.

She nodded, again acknowledging the tragic event that had left the twins orphaned. Sawyer had told her his father—widowed? divorced?—had remarried and started a late-in-life family.

"How are the boys doing? Emotionally, I mean." She didn't want to get in over her head. "I'm not a psychologist or counselor, if that's what you're looking for."

"What I'm after is a competent pair of eyes and ears—and someone who's good with kids. Your friend Sunshine assures me you took good care of her daughter while she was wrapped up in the town council campaign last fall. That you and Tessa have a good relationship."

"I've known Tess since she was a baby, so that could account for that."

"You're being too modest. Sunshine mentioned you grew up babysitting neighbor kids, as well."

"I did." That had been the only means of earning money for her artistic endeavors until she was old enough to work in one of the tourist-frequented shops. Infant care had scared her, but by the time her charges reached the toddler stage she'd done fine. Okay, maybe better than fine.

"Sunshine says you're bright, well-grounded, sensible

and loyal to a fault," he continued, making her sound like the next best thing to a golden retriever. "She says, too, that if you err, it's on the side of caution. That's what I need. Someone I can entrust with my little brothers."

She looked at him doubtfully, uneasiness continuing to gnaw as he handed her a slip of paper with the Selbys' phone number and email address. "You're telling me, then, that you don't know anyone else in town who fits the bill?"

The pretty blonde with gray eyes and a pixie haircut was sharp alright, homing in on that point. Truth was, in addition to her other job-suitable assets, Tori was relatively new to town. Having lived here off and on for under six months, it appeared she hadn't yet formed deep attachments aside from the established one with Sunshine. She wouldn't be attuned to the histories of those who lived here—like his—and wouldn't be likely to make assumptions or confide in others. She was a churchgoer, too, which would win persuasive points with his siblings' grandparents during an interview. A solid recommendation from a past and present pastor and any former employers would further strengthen her prospects.

"Truth of the matter is, Tori, I've known Sunshine for several years and the family she's marrying into even longer, and she highly recommends you. I personally don't know anyone else who appears to meet the needs of the situation I've found myself in. I've never before had to be a nanny recruiter."

He offered what he hoped was a winning smile, but Tori made a face.

"*Please* don't call the position nanny." Color rose in her cheeks, almost matching the soft pink of her turtleneck sweater. "That word always makes me picture a goat herding—pardon the pun—kids."

He managed not to laugh as his spirits lifted at the cute expression on her face. He'd have to watch himself if she'd be working here as well as with his brothers. He couldn't afford to let himself get distracted right now, not with the Outpost needing his full attention. He couldn't put his livelihood at further risk by not giving his best to keep it afloat. And he certainly couldn't risk it for what would in all probability be another here-today-gone-tomorrow relationship. But she'd obviously taken exception to the nanny label. Might that mean she was seriously considering his offer?

"Then *nanny* is tossed out the door. Babysitter? Caregiver? Childcare worker?"

"Much better."

After rising from his chair, he moved around to the front of the desk and sat on the edge of it. "What other questions do you have?"

If he wasn't mistaken, he needed to come across as open and approachable, especially considering her reservations about the possibility of being involved in a custody battle. He honestly didn't want to be part of anything like that any more than she did. No way. What would he do with two little kids underfoot? Children were time-consuming. Demanded attention. With him being next in line for legal guardianship, per the wishes of the boys' parents, he hoped with all his heart that Therese and Ray were perfectly capable of raising his little brothers. If investing a few extra bucks in hired help increased that likelihood and kept him out of direct oversight of the twins, it would be money well spent. And if that hired help provided him an inside line to the household dynamics, all the better.

A crease formed between Tori's brows as she looked around his office, then toward the door that led to the main room of the business he'd inherited from his grandfather right out of college. Hunting, fishing, camping and hiking paraphernalia packed the rustic interior of a building that faced the winding, pine-lined main road through town.

"This other part-time job you mentioned," she said, focusing again on him. "The one here. What would that entail? I'm not sure I'm the right fit for clerking in a place like this. I don't know anything about hunting or fishing and not much more about camping, although I've hiked."

"There you go. And you've rung up a sale on a cash register before?"

"In shops that I worked at in Jerome, yes. But—"

"You wouldn't have to advise someone on purchases. Les, Diego or I'll be around to do that." He hesitated, then brushed back the hair from his eyes and gave her an apologetic look. "It's not glamorous, but in addition to stocking, inventory and general office work, I could use assistance with upkeep."

"You mean housekeeping, right? Not toolbox types of stuff, but dusting and cleaning and that kind of thing?"

"Right."

To his relief she merely shrugged, unfazed. Hopes mounting, he hurried on. "Depending on the schedule you arrange with the Selbys, you can work your hours in around here as you find most convenient."

She tilted her head slightly. "That's assuming, of course, that I get the childcare job. *If* I decide to apply, I mean."

His rising spirits faltered. "Right."

"How many hours a week are we talking about?"

"That depends on what you agree to with Ray and

Therese. Assuming it's at least twenty hours a week there, I could probably make up the difference on this end to bring it up to a total of thirty-five or forty."

That sounded plenty generous to him and probably more than he could afford right now. But he caught uncertainty in her eyes. "Is there a problem?"

"Well, I do have a business of my own that I'd hoped to get off the ground after a too-long sabbatical."

"I wasn't aware of that."

"Not that I'm not looking for a job," she said quickly. "I am. But I'm also trying to use the months before summer to prepare a body of work for the Hunter Ridge Artists' Cooperative."

He knew from Sunshine that Tori hailed from Jerome, Arizona, an old mining town turned artists' colony and tourist attraction. So last night he'd touched base with the mother of a friend who lived there. She'd mentioned— among other things—Tori's involvement in the arts. Although one reported incident from Tori's teen years might make the Selbys leery of hiring her, nothing about it alarmed him. She was still a top-notch candidate.

"I'm a quilter." She met his gaze almost cautiously, as if watching for his reaction. "Not only bedspreads and comforters, but wall hangings and other home and office decorations. Pillows, purses and tote bags, too."

That sounded practical enough. Unpretentious. "My mom always wanted to quilt. Never had time, though, with three rambunctious boys."

He didn't miss the curiosity that flickered through her eyes, but he wasn't wading into the past today. Then he glanced down at the photo of the twins, a professional picture taken not too long before their parents died. Maybe it was his imagination, but the boys seemed increasingly subdued lately, not as lively and laughter-filled as they'd once been. Was that to be expected with the loss of their folks—or was it related to something in their current living environment?

He had his suspicions. And since they'd still be living happily with their parents if he'd have taken care of business, his mission now was to see to their welfare. But time was running out on this particular opportunity. He'd learned yesterday that Ray and Therese had placed a want ad in surrounding-area church newsletters two weeks ago and were embarking on a search for a part-time live-in helper.

He motioned to the photo. "So, are you interested in the childcare position? Interviews are under way, and although I don't anticipate a quick decision on their part, timing is critical to get your application in. If filling in here also is too much to take on, we can figure something out."

He'd intended it, though, to serve as a perfect means of discreetly keeping in touch concerning the boys.

She stood, then reached for her coat and a colorful quilted handbag—one she'd no doubt made. Expressive eyes met his, and he held his breath.

Come on, say yes.

"Thanks for your time—Sawyer." She offered an apologetic smile. "But I'll need to think about it. Give me twenty-four hours."

"I guess tomorrow night is Sunshine and Grady's big event." Benton Mason, a bearded silversmith, held the door open for Tori to exit the Hunter Ridge Artists' Co-operative, where he, like other members of the co-op, worked part-time.

Hopefully she'd be joining those artists in the not-too-distant future. As soon, that is, as she could pull together the best sampling of her work for submission to the co-op's jury for evaluation and, if given the nod, complete a probationary period. Which made it all the more important that she focus on bringing her skills back up to speed so she wouldn't miss out on the summer tourist-season shoppers.

"Theirs is a match made in Heaven, for sure," she chimed in cheerfully enough. But if there was anything she could do without today, it was a reminder that her best friend would wed on Valentine's Day in an intimate family-and-close-friends ceremony. And also the related reminder that she had barely two weeks before she had to be out of the apartment above the Hunter Ridge Artists' Cooperative, where she'd resided with Sunshine and her daughter since early last autumn.

While Tori's friend would be moving to Grady's cabin at Hunter's Hideaway, his family's enterprise catering to outdoor enthusiasts, Sunshine had hoped to hang on to the apartment awhile longer so Tori would have a roof over her head until at least summer. But co-op members voted to lease the space starting next month and, unfortunately, a jobless Tori couldn't afford the apartment.

"Any employment nibbles, Tori?" With sympathetic eyes, Benton stood in the open doorway.

"A few." None, unfortunately, looked half as promising as what Sawyer Banks had proposed yesterday afternoon, which happened to include an apartment at the Selbys' place.

But the thought of being Sawyer's undercover operative still left a bad taste in her mouth. Although she'd prayed about it nonstop, she still didn't have an answer. She'd told him, though, that she'd give him a response within twenty-four hours.

Two hours to go.

"Lizzie and I can let you stay at our place for a while." Benton gave her a reassuring smile. "Things would be tight with five kids under our roof, but we could manage."

"Thanks, but I have reason to hope things will come together soon."

"I know you don't want to go back to Jerome, even though it's much more of a thriving arts community than Hunter Ridge."

"No." Not back to where Grandma had passed away two years ago and where Heath Davidson, her former fiancé, still resided. As the old saying went, the town wasn't big enough for the both of them. After the breakup last fall, she'd given up the rental house she'd shared with her grandma Eriksen, ready to shake off the past.

"It will work out." She feigned a confident smile. "But I'd better let you get back to work."

Snugging her coat collar, she started past the cluster of businesses running along the snowplowed blacktopped road, flurries frolicking in the air around her. It hadn't taken long to adapt to the cooler high-elevation town with its towering ponderosa pines and frequent winter snowfalls. Whenever feasible, she ran errands on foot, not bothering with negotiating snow-packed roads in her blue Kia compact.

The crisp, pine-scented mountain air energized her as she made her way down the street, but as she approached Bealer's Ice Cream Emporium her steps slowed. She'd seen an ad in the weekly paper that Pete Bealer was looking for a Saturday manager starting in May. That came too late to boost her finances enough to swing the co-op apartment, but maybe if she could line up several part-time jobs, she could afford a room somewhere.

When Pastor Garrett McCrae married Jodi Thorpe, he'd be moving out of the space he rented in the home of church members. But that wouldn't be available until the first weekend in May, assuming they'd be willing to rent to her, too. In two weeks she could be living out of her car unless she applied for and got the childcare position.

But despite Sunshine's encouragement when they'd talked last night, wouldn't she feel like a dirty rotten sneak prying into the relationship some unsuspecting couple had with their grandsons? Sawyer seemed sincere enough, though, when insisting he had no intention of snatching the kids from them. In fact, Sunshine laughed when Tori had confessed that suspicion to her.

Sawyer Banks? she'd said, her eyes wide with disbelief. *You think he'd willingly take little kids into his freewheeling bachelor life? Get real.*

If only she had more options.

It is what it is, sweetheart. She could almost hear Grandma Eriksen's chuckle. How many times had Gran reminded her that half the turmoil she put herself through revolved around pushing against reality and resisting a situation in which she wished she hadn't found herself? Wasting time bemoaning rather than buckling down and digging out? If only Grandma were still here to talk to...

Great. There she went again. Denying reality.

With rekindled determination, she stepped inside the old-fashioned ice cream parlor, where she was brought up short by an earsplitting wail.

"I want my mommy!" a child gasped in what she guessed to be the middle of a crying jag.

A slightly familiar-looking man seated in a high-backed booth glanced at her apologetically. Then with renewed resolve, he refocused on the youngster she couldn't see seated across from him.

"If you want me to take you home without ice cream,

I can do that." The gray-haired man's voice remained low. Kind, but firm.

The child wailed again, louder, reinforcing that he wanted his mommy.

"We both know that's impossible. Now sit up and act like the big boy that you are."

"Mommy!"

The man glanced uncomfortably in the direction of Emporium owner Pete Bealer, who looked on with a pained expression. The couple he was serving shook their heads in commiseration. That was all it took to bring the older man to his feet as he pulled on his coat. Then he held out his hand to the unseen child.

"Come along, then."

"Nooooo!"

The man finally leaned in to gently drag the resisting child out of the booth and set him on his feet. The boy, still turned away from her, stared down at the floor, his shoulders shaking with sobs. Poor little guy.

"Now settle down," the older man admonished. "You know big boys don't cry."

A knee-buckling chill raced through Tori.

Stop it. Stop it right now, Victoria. You know big girls don't cry.

If a bolt of lightning had crashed at her feet, it couldn't have startled her more than the intrusion of her father's voice as she mentally hurtled back in time.

I'm very disappointed in you, young lady.

Prying her away from him, her father had concluded his condemning statement with a rough shake, displeasure written on his youthful face. He had been leaving them. Leaving Mommy. Leaving her. And he was angry because she'd clung to him and cried as he headed to the door.

"Now stop it, Cubby." The man's voice jerked her back to the present.

Cubby?

Stunned, she looked to where the man she assumed to be the boy's grandfather had gotten the sobbing child into his coat and lifted the boy into his arms. Gave him a hug.

The blond boy met her gaze with a plaintive, tear-stained face and bluer-than-blue eyes.

Eyes like his twin's?

Like those of his older half brother?

Shaken, she offered him an encouraging smile, then watched as grandfather and grandson exited the ice cream shop.

"Miss?" the shop's owner called out. "Sit anywhere you'd like, and I'll be with you in a minute."

"Um, no, thanks. I've changed my mind about…ice cream."

She waved a distracted farewell, then stepped outside where snow now descended in earnest.

She had her answer.

It would only take a quick minute to phone the Selbys and express her interest in the caregiver position. Then if given the go-ahead to apply, tomorrow she'd submit a résumé and solicit letters of recommendation.

Pulling up her hood against the buffeting wind, Tori headed in the direction of her apartment, the broken-hearted sobs of a little boy—*and a little girl*—still echo-ing in her ears.

Chapter Two

"Welcome, Tori." Ray Selby smiled as he opened the front door to the imposing two-story stone house at seven o'clock on a Thursday morning. Incredibly, it was only a week after she'd interviewed and been offered the job.

"You know, though," he added drily as he motioned her inside the shadowed entryway, "you *could* use that key Therese gave you. You don't have to ring the bell. You're part of this household now."

"I know, but I thought the first time I should at least announce myself. You know, before Grady and Luke Hunter come traipsing in behind me with furniture and the rest of my stuff."

Ray glanced toward the street where her friend Sunshine's new husband, Grady, and his older brother were waiting by Luke's loaded crew-cab pickup. They and Sunshine had gone with her to Jerome yesterday to retrieve belongings stored in a friend's garage. She'd enjoyed reliving highlights of last week's wedding and hearing about the newlyweds' stay at the Grand Canyon's El Tovar Hotel, right on the rim. She'd appreciated, too, their support as she returned to the town she'd felt compelled to leave some months ago.

Thankfully, she hadn't seen her ex-fiancé on the streets that were, by contrast to summer's bustling tourist season, fairly deserted this time of year. How could she have been so mistaken as to have believed they'd be a good match?

Ray waved Luke and Grady forward and they leaped into action, lowering the tailgate and carefully unloading her grandmother's blanket-swathed antique dresser.

The older man continued to smile at her as the others approached. "I can't tell you how thankful Therese and I are that you said yes to our offer. Especially after the show Cubby and I treated you to at the Ice Cream Emporium. It was a relief that you didn't scare easily."

"It takes more than an unhappy little boy to run me off."

On the contrary, it had won her over.

With Tori leading the way past a small library on one side of the spacious hallway and what she could only think of as a parlor on the other, she and the men skirted past a sweeping staircase and a darkened dining room. Another hall branched off, leading to a rear corner of the house and what had once been a cook-housekeeper's apartment, and would now be her new home. At least for a few years anyway, if all went well.

"This is nice." Luke sounded surprised as the brothers carefully lowered the dresser to the spot she indicated.

When given the grand tour following her interview she, too, had been pleasantly surprised to find the apartment featured a kitchenette, sleeping alcove, walk-in closet and its own bathroom. Lots of sunshine-filled windows, as well. Although the space was furnished, Ray had had the bed frame and dresser moved elsewhere so she could bring her grandmother's antiques.

They'd barely finished hauling in the remainder of her

belongings, reattaching the mirror to the dresser and getting the bed set up and mattress placed, when the chatter of children echoed down the hallway from the front of the house.

"Sounds like the troops are up and on the move." Ray gave Tori a wary glance. "Brace yourself."

Since tomorrow would be her actual first day on the job, she'd hoped for time to get settled in today. Oh, well.

"Hey, look what I found!"

They turned to see Sawyer Banks in the doorway, holding a grinning twin in each arm—no small feat, since they must weigh at least forty pounds each. Tori almost gasped at the resemblance between the threesome. The mussed blond hair. Blue eyes. Matching smiles.

But what was Sawyer doing here? Checking up on her? Reminding her that she had an obligation to him? If so, he wasn't going to like what she'd be sharing as soon as the opportunity presented itself.

"Which one of you boys let *this* character in?" Ray teased his grandsons. Or maybe that gruffness and the sharp look in Sawyer's direction wasn't teasing? When she'd let the Selbys know she'd be working at the Outpost part-time, they'd raised no objections, and Sawyer had told her he had a "decent enough" relationship with his brothers and their grandparents. That was clearly evident in the case of the obviously excited boys, but was it her imagination that there was tension hanging in the air between the two men?

"He brought us a new game." Cubby waved a small box in the air as if to legitimize opening the door to him.

Their big brother gave them a hug, then set their feet on the floor. The pair were dressed in tennies, jeans and sweatshirts, and side by side the resemblance between them was evident, although not identical. Cubby's face was less rounded than Landon's and devoid of the few freckles that scattered across his brother's nose. Nor was his gaze as bold. And whereas Landon's reddish-tinted bangs fell evenly across his forehead, Cubby's hair had a definite side part.

Both thrust their hands into their back pockets, a mirror image of each other—and of Sawyer's stance behind them.

"Say good-morning to Tori," Ray prompted, apparently mindful that she'd soon be an instrumental player in the lives of his grandsons.

"Good morning, Tori," all three Banks brothers responded. Landon confidently. Cubby, with his head ducked shyly. Sawyer with mischief dancing in his eyes.

Why did her heart pirouette when she met Sawyer's gaze? Not good. "Good morning, *boys*."

"Now that Banks is here—after the work's done— looks like you're finished with us." Luke glanced around the room with satisfaction, then Tori walked the Hunter brothers to the door, reiterating her thanks. When she returned, Ray had vanished, but Sawyer and the boys were unabashedly exploring her new living quarters.

She'd assumed contact with Sawyer would be strictly during her work hours at the Outpost—although they hadn't yet established those days or hours. If he popped in frequently to see Cubby and Landon, why was he in need of an "inside line" to the household?

"Sawyer, look." Landon pointed at something inside the open door of a lower kitchenette cabinet. "That's a mousetrap."

Wonderful.

Sawyer squatted next to him. "Sure is, buddy. But there's nothing in it, so that's a good sign. Probably put there as a precaution since this apartment's been empty for a while."

Did he believe that, or was he throwing out that reassurance for her benefit?

"Let me see." Cubby pushed his brother aside and squished in beside Sawyer to duck down and look, too. "Wouldn't it be cool to see a mouse in it?"

Sawyer cast an amused look in her direction. "You'd rather not, right?"

"I could do without one."

Landon looked up hopefully as he wandered away to peek in the walk-in closet. "But we could catch it and keep it as a pet. We don't have any pets."

"We don't have pets because G'ma is 'lergic." Cubby gave a solemn nod. "Maybe she's 'lergic to mouses, too."

His twin sneered. "Nobody's allergic to mice, stupid."

"Landon." She caught the boy's eye and shook her head. "Your brother isn't stupid. Please don't call him that."

He shrugged. "It's scientifically proven mice aren't big enough and don't have enough dander to cause an allergic reaction."

Cubby frowned. "What's dander?"

"Icky stuff that gets in your hair." Eyes widening and brows elevated, Landon lifted his hands over his head as he stalked toward his brother. "Creepy crawly stuff with hairy legs and tiny teeth."

Sawyer grabbed him and pulled him in close to noogie the top of his head. "And maybe you're full of hot air."

The giggling boy pulled away.

The teasing part she could live with, but the questionable "scientifically proven" bit, spoken with an air of authority, she'd have to be on the alert for.

"Landon? Cubby?" a feminine voice called from the open doorway. "Time for breakfast."

"Good morning, Therese." Tori smiled at the dark-haired, stylishly coifed woman dressed in wool slacks, a blue cashmere sweater and low pumps. From the information Sawyer had provided, she must be in her mid-seventies; Ray about that age, as well.

"Good morning, Victoria—Tori." As Cubby snatched up their new game from the top of the bed and the boys dashed past her to the kitchen, she leveled her gaze on Sawyer. "Good morning to you, too. Ray mentioned you'd stopped by. We haven't seen you in quite a while."

"The Outpost keeps me hopping."

"The Outpost. Yes, I imagine so." She turned again to Tori. "I'll do my best to keep the boys out of your hair today. I imagine you'll want to unpack and find a home for your things."

"That would be wonderful. Thanks."

"Have you had breakfast?"

Tori noticed she didn't include Sawyer in the query. "Before the crack of dawn, but thanks for asking."

"Do plan to join us for lunch. Eleven thirty."

"I'll do that."

Still standing in the doorway, Therese briefly touched her fingertips to the door's polished wood, then raised a delicate brow at Tori. "You do recall our house rules?"

Ah, yes. The apartment door should remain open at all times when hosting male guests.

"I do. Thank you."

While Tori hadn't dated since Heath's departure, she was in no hurry to again, so that wouldn't be a problem. But although Sawyer's unexpected presence wasn't anything close to a date, she wasn't convinced either Ray or

Therese was particularly pleased with his putting in an appearance on her first day in their household.

Which didn't exactly reflect the lay of the land that Sawyer had led her to believe.

Leave it to Therese to put him in his place in front of Tori. But what had he expected? He'd made himself scarce, then here he came barging back into their lives bearing gifts right smack on the day they'd acquired a new—and attractive—nanny.

No, not nanny. Childcare giver.

When the twins' grandmother departed, he snagged a couple of paper towels from the dispenser above the counter. "Let me get that mousetrap out of here. You'll want to clean the cabinet and put stuff in there."

"But if there are mice…"

He reached into the back of the cabinet with a paper towel and pulled out the trap. Inspected it. Wrapped it up, then stood. "The cheese is hardened. It's been there for quite a while with no takers. Ray probably forgot it was under there."

She gave him a relieved smile. "That's good."

He glanced at the door still open to the hallway, amused at Therese's unsubtle allusion to "house rules"—as if she thought he'd attempt to put the moves on Tori if left alone behind closed doors?

While Tori had called to let him know she'd applied for and then gotten the job, he hadn't seen her since early last week, and she looked prettier this morning than he remembered. Pale blond hair framed her face, accentuating expressive eyes, and that smile she'd flashed in his direction a time or two made his breath catch. Was that why he'd shown up on her doorstep this morning with the excuse of dropping off a new game for the boys?

He looked down at the wrapped mousetrap in his hand, then back at Tori. "I don't suppose you noticed that Landon can stretch the truth if it suits his purposes?"

Invented. Fabricated. Made-up. Nobody liked you to use the blunt word *liar* these days.

"I did notice. To my knowledge, science hasn't proven anything of the sort as he claimed. I have no doubt there *are* people who are allergic to mice."

"That's something he's gotten into since coming to live here. He cites studies or claims he saw it on some TV documentary. Makes it sound real legit. If you didn't know better...well, you'd swallow it hook, line and sinker."

"Why do you think he does it?" She looked at him earnestly, as if expecting him to have all the answers.

"I expect, for the most part, to buffalo his brother. There's some competition there. Maybe he thinks he can win Therese's and Ray's approval, too."

"Do they call him on that behavior?"

"I imagine they do when they catch him at it. I'm glad you picked up on it right away."

He'd had the wool pulled over his own eyes more than a few times until Landon started in about some "fact" related to trapshooting that had absolutely no basis in reality. But he'd *sounded* so credible, knowledgeable, and someone who wasn't a trapshooter would have let it slide by.

"I'll make it a priority to work with Therese and Ray to get that habit nipped in the bud." She frowned slightly, as if this issue was something he should have made her aware of in advance. "Is there anything I need to know about Cubby?"

"Nothing of that nature." Or at least he didn't think there was. But it wasn't as if he'd seen the boys on a regular basis since their parents had died. Only enough to know that they weren't fully the same kids they'd been a year ago. Which was why it would be good to have Tori here, an objective observer. "He can get emotional. Tends to play Therese with tears, which irritates Ray to no end."

She nodded, but didn't look surprised. Had she seen some of that during her interview and follow-up meetings with the Selbys?

"So," he said, determined to broach the next subject. "Do you have a feel for when you might start at the Outpost?"

"Would you mind awfully much if I got through a week here before we make that decision? It may take a while to determine what schedule works best for the boys, the Selbys and me."

While he needed her to start deep cleaning and organizing at the Outpost as soon as possible, readying the place for what he hoped would be a busy season, that would be one less week he'd have to pay her.

"Okay, then, we'll talk a week from now."

"Which brings up something else you need to know…" She lifted her chin slightly, as if expecting to be challenged on whatever she was about to say. With a glance to the open door, she lowered her voice. "I won't be accepting your proposed dollar addition to the hourly wage the Selbys offered."

He drew a quick breath. She was holding out for more? He hadn't anticipated an underhanded maneuver like that.

"I'm not sure I understand," he said carefully, "what you mean, Tori."

She clasped her hands together, looking more sweetness and light than the hardheaded negotiator she apparently was. "It simply means that I won't accept monetary compensation that obligates me to you. Not beyond, I mean, what you pay me as your employee at the Outpost."

"Hold on a minute." She wasn't asking for more money, she was ditching her "obligation" to him altogether? "I thought when we last spoke that you understood—"

"That you were buying my services as a snitch?" Her smile was entirely too perky. "I understood that clearly, Mr. Banks. Which is why I *almost* walked away from this job opportunity you presented. That is, until I had time to rethink a few things."

He frowned. He'd been snookered.

To his irritation, she laughed. "Don't worry. I'll look out for the twins and it won't cost you a dime. Think of me as a human smoke detector. If there's anything that concerns me about the safety or welfare of Cubby and Landon, I'll quietly sound the alarm."

"But you won't be—?"

"Reporting to you? Nope." She shrugged, as if that settled it.

His gaze flickered to the open door to ensure they were still alone.

"But…" Despite his reluctance to make an issue of something he'd picked up from his friend's mother, he couldn't help countering her smile with one of his own. "I can make sure the Selbys won't retain you for long."

Wariness lit her eyes. "Why would you want to do that?"

"Could be I'm not entirely sure you're trustworthy." He folded his arms. "Surely you don't think I'd recruit you to look after my brothers if I didn't do my homework, do you?"

As realization dawned, her pretty mouth dropped open with a sound of protest. "I can explain. That was a long time ago. And I was only—"

"Seventeen. I'm confident nothing of that nature will

ever happen again. But the Selbys are quite conservative, you know, and getting arrested for trespassing and disturbing the peace might not sit well with them. A potentially bad influence on their grandsons."

A multitude of emotions sparked in her eyes. Lips now pressed together, she looked momentarily down at the floor, most likely gathering her thoughts. Then back at him.

"Court records for a minor would have been sealed. So how did you...?"

"You're not the only one who has friends in Jerome."

Her eyes narrowed. "You've known this all along but are going to use it now to throw a roadblock in my working here? I'm serious that I'll involve you if I feel something jeopardizes the boys."

"You need this job, though, don't you?" he said softly, watching her closely. Apparently, from what he'd learned from his friend's mother, a relationship breakup was what had sent her flying to Hunter Ridge in the first place, and he doubted she'd want to return to her hometown if she could make a go of it elsewhere. "You need the housing benefit, too, if you intend to stay here."

"I— Yes, of course, I need both housing and a job. I've made no secret of that. But I don't want to feel like an informer on people with whom I'm building a relationship. People I'll be living with under the same roof." She folded her arms, a reflection of his own stance. "And if you put in a bad word for me with the Selbys, in a small town like this whatever you tell them could get around. Make it difficult for me to find another job."

He had her now. "It could."

For a long moment, she dared to glare daggers at him. But when her expression abruptly softened, his gut tightened in uneasy anticipation of her next response.

"The other day you as good as said you didn't have any viable alternate candidates," she said smoothly, watching him like a kitten at a mouse hole. "I got the impression I was your last hope."

She had him there—and had the nerve to smile at that insight. It was true he didn't know anyone else in town who might be sympathetic enough—and discreet enough—to help him out. Or at least no one who'd be available for childcare duties.

"So where does this leave us?" Tori's challenging stance eased as she unfolded her arms, apparently assured that she'd played the winning hand.

He had to hand it to her. She had pluck.

While he could be pigheaded here because she refused to cooperate with him across the board, that would be cutting off his nose to spite his face. He *needed* her in the kids' household.

He squinted one eye. "A compromise?"

"We both have a horse in this race, don't we?"

"Guess we do."

"Bottom line, though, is that, outside of my work at the Outpost, I don't want to take money from you or to otherwise be obligated to report to you." She quirked an engaging smile. "So take it or leave it."

Chapter Three

Even to her own ears, that didn't sound like much of a compromise on her part.

And standing her ground was a risk—a foolhardy one perhaps—given that Sawyer had exercised due diligence before recruiting her. While she could explain the situation to any reasonable person—she and a group of high school friends had staged a protest when an out-of-town developer managed to circumvent local laws and was preparing to raze a historic building—Sawyer was right. The Selbys might not take an arrest lightly.

Nor did it sound as if he'd be interested in hearing her side of the story. Besides, didn't Grandma always say wrong is wrong, and having a reason for doing it didn't make it right?

Sawyer's assessing gaze locked on hers as she held her breath, preparing for another reminder that with a few well-chosen words he could ensure she wouldn't retain this job—or land any other job in town, for that matter.

But he didn't respond. At all.

"So," she said hesitantly as the silence stretched between them. "You're good with that?"

"It looks as if I'll have to be, doesn't it? That is, as

long as you alert me to anything significant that could negatively impact my brothers."

"You have my word on it."

"And you have mine to keep my mouth shut, as well. Assuming, of course…"

"I said you have my word."

He nodded. But despite the grudging settlement between them, she held no illusions that he was pleased about this turn of events. Even though they'd only recently become acquainted, it was clear Sawyer Banks wasn't a man who liked to have his plans thwarted.

Nevertheless, a prayer of thanks winged its way Heavenward. Sawyer didn't seem to personally hold her teenage infractions against her and had agreed not to share them with the Selbys as long as she kept her part of the bargain.

She wanted this job. How often in the past week had she relived her encounter with the orphaned Cubby and his grandfather at the ice cream shop? Recalled how it had hit too close to home? She wanted to be here for the little guy and his brother. She *needed* to be here to hold them and hug them when tears flowed. But she had no intention of sharing with Sawyer her impressions of that chance—or divine?—meeting or what convinced her to change her mind about applying for the job.

He wouldn't understand.

"What did Ray and Therese say—" Sawyer's gaze probed "—when you told them you'd also be working part-time at the Outpost?"

He hadn't initially been pleased last week when she insisted that she'd tell them before accepting any job offer. "They were good with it."

He looked at her doubtfully.

She didn't attempt to elaborate. Couldn't, in fact, because there was nothing else to tell except that Therese and Ray had exchanged a look, the significance of which she didn't understand. Then Ray nodded and thanked her for telling them.

That was it.

So why did Sawyer seem to think they might not be pleased?

"Is there something you're not telling me about your relationship with the Selbys?"

"What makes you think that?"

"You weren't thrilled when I told you I was going to be up front with them about plans to work for you, and now you're doubting me when I told you they didn't have any problems with it. Obviously, you anticipated they might."

"What can I say? It's awkward. You know, their daughter being married to my dad. Me being a half brother to the product of that union. Me being an age most would expect the twins' father to be. I'm part of the family, yet not really. It's hard to figure out how I'm supposed to fit into the boys' lives. Into Therese's and Ray's."

She could see how that connection would be a problematic one, for the Selbys and Sawyer alike. Definitely complex. Maybe that's all there was to the tension she'd sensed this morning. Nothing more.

Ready to move away from unsettling topics, she nodded to the wad of paper towels in his hand, her nose wrinkling. "Thanks for disposing of *that*. I hope I won't need it."

He laughed. "Naw. I think you'll be fine."

"I'll remind myself of your words if I hear any rustling in the kitchen during the deep dark hours of the night."

He lifted his hand that held the trap. "Call me. Any hour. Day or night. I'll be on your doorstep."

Her cheeks warmed as their gazes met.

"I'd better get going." He moved toward the door to the hallway. "I have errands to run before I open up shop this morning and I need to let you get to your unpacking."

"Lots to do." She motioned to the stacks of boxes. "I guess I'll talk to you next week, then?"

"Sounds like a plan."

Yeah, it was a plan alright. That is, unless she needed the mousetrap reset after all...

Sawyer had barely climbed into his crew-cab pickup when his cell phone rang. He glanced at the caller ID, then grimaced. Kyle Guthridge.

"Yo, Sawyer." His friend's west Texas drawl echoed in his ear despite the fact the man had lived in Arizona since he was twelve. "Got your phone message that you'll be late on tomorrow's payment."

At least he had the generosity of spirit not to say "again." Sawyer cringed inwardly, acutely aware of the risk his longtime friend had knowingly taken in extending the loan, probably one his wife had loudly protested.

"My apologies, Kyle. Temporary cash-flow problem. But I'll be able to make a deposit by the end of next week and will drop off a check then."

"I totally get the cash-flow issue and don't mean to badger you."

"It won't happen again." But this was the second time in four months. He prided himself on his integrity. His financial responsibility. But since early last summer he'd been hammered by one unbudgeted expense after another, most related to building maintenance. Plumbing. Electrical. And who'd have thought a new roof and replacing a furnace large enough for a retail space would cost that much?

That series of events had led him to approach a few

buddies for personal loans rather than the bank where he'd taken over Grandpa's mortgage payments on the Outpost. But he'd sell his pop-up camper or his fishing boat before he'd allow a payment to be delayed a third time.

"You're not badgering," Sawyer continued, embarrassed for his friend at having to speak up as much as he was for himself. "We're friends, but we're also businessmen."

"That we are." Kyle paused. "I don't suppose you're going to the play at the church next Friday night, are you? Annie and I are taking the kids. Family friendly. You could bring the check with you. That would save you a trip to my place."

Kyle lived a distance out of town, off a branching series of dirt roads that weren't well maintained in the winter months. But a church play geared toward youngsters? Not exactly high on his couldn't-wait-to-do list.

"I won't be able to swing that, but you'll have your check on Friday. Guaranteed." He wouldn't drop the check off in advance of making the deposit, though. Kyle had been known to get preoccupied—okay, absentminded, to be more accurate—and giving it to him early could risk premature cashing and bouncing of the check. "Thanks for the extension."

"You're welcome, buddy. Have a good rest of your week."

Sawyer repocketed his cell phone and stared down the snowy street. Winter was still wreaking havoc with his bottom line, but by late spring he should see an uptick in demand for outdoor gear. Continuing to tighten the rein on everything but the most necessary expenses for the next six or seven months might allow him, by autumn, to get that personal loan paid off.

Was it a wise move, then, to employ Tori part-time right now? While she'd help out behind the scenes, by her own admission she didn't know anything about hunting, fishing or camping. But with her hired to take care of his brothers, he needed to uphold his part of the bargain. Make sure it was monetarily worth her while to remain in Hunter Ridge.

He owed his dad and his dad's wife that much. And the boys.

He'd come up with the money.

Somehow.

He started up the truck and headed in the direction of the Outpost. As Therese had mentioned, he hadn't visited Cubby and Landon in a while. But he wasn't sure how welcome he was. Like he'd told Tori, it was an awkward situation.

What he *hadn't* shared, though, was that he couldn't help fearing that Dad's wife may have told her parents that Sawyer had promised her he'd take care of things while Dad was out of town. Feared they were silently watching, waiting for a confession that their daughter's death was his fault. But they'd been on an Alaskan cruise the week of the fire and, gradually, he'd come to realize it was unlikely that Vanessa had contacted them about what at the time seemed a trivial matter. But that didn't ease the guilt when he was around them.

Who'd ever heard of a hot water heater blowing up and catching a house on fire?

When she walked into church Friday night a week later, Tori couldn't help but remember the first time she'd stepped through the doors with her friend Sunshine last autumn—Labor Day weekend. She marveled at how far she'd come since then.

Emotionally battered and bruised, still in shock at the unexpected turn of events with her fiancé, she'd been drawn in by the brown-brick edifice with its old-fashioned bell tower and stained glass windows. Now, greeting those around her and helping the twins into a pew near the front where they could best see the play, she felt right at home. Knowing, too, that she'd helped design and sew tonight's costumes for the high school–aged actors gave her an even greater sense of belonging.

Amazingly she had an almost stranger, Sawyer Banks, to thank that she'd be able to remain in town after all.

"Why are you smiling, Tori?" Cubby stared up at her intently as she helped him out of his coat. "What's funny?"

"Not funny," she whispered, banishing the image of Sawyer that lingered in her mind. "I'm just happy."

About things having nothing whatsoever to do with Sawyer, of course.

"I'm happy, too," he whispered back.

"You are? Why is that?"

"Because I like church. Landon and I used to come here with our mommy and daddy when we were little. They're in Heaven now." His forehead creased as he gazed up at a stained glass window of Christ walking along a rocky road, a staff in one hand and a lamb cradled in His other arm. "Did you know my mommy and daddy?"

"No, I didn't. I wish I had."

He settled back into the pew. "I miss them."

She patted his hand. "I know you do."

"Hey, look!" Cubby's twin cried out in a too-loud-for-church voice. But fortunately others were still finding seats and no one seemed to notice. "It's Sawyer. See?"

Tori and Cubby both turned to look where Landon

was pointing. Sure enough, Sawyer was standing inside the main door, visually searching the growing crowd and looking, if she weren't mistaken, slightly desperate.

"I bet he's trying to find us." Landon scooted out of the pew and Tori made a grab for him, but he escaped by mere inches and headed up the middle aisle toward the rear of the sanctuary. At least she managed to detain Cubby, who'd also slid out of the wooden seat. He was attempting to squeeze past her knees, which she'd pressed against the pew in front of them.

"Stay here, Cubby." But how could she retrieve Landon and keep his brother corralled at the same time?

"We gotta get Sawyer, Tori. With all these people, he can't see us."

She wasn't convinced Sawyer was there to find the boys. He looked more like a man on a mission who wanted nothing more than to get in and back out as quickly as possible.

Then an unexpected apprehension stabbed. Had something happened to Therese and Ray and he *was* here to find her and his brothers? She'd offered to take the boys to the church play so the couple could gather with friends in Canyon Springs, a town about thirty minutes away. It would be, Therese had confided before they departed several hours ago, one of a few out-of-town evenings without the children that they'd managed since taking the boys into their lives full-time.

Queasiness roiled her stomach as she stood, hoping Sawyer would spot her. Unfortunately, Cubby used the opportunity to squirt past her and into the aisle. She caught his arm. "Hold on a minute."

She glanced back at their coats and her purse on the pew. Surely no one here would bother them, would they?

Then Cubby grasped her hand and tugged. "Okay, I'm coming."

Like fish swimming upstream, they wove between the arriving playgoers, and up ahead she could see Landon in earnest discussion with his big brother and pointing toward the front of the church. Sawyer, on the other hand, was shaking his head and looking around him, apparently still in search of an elusive someone. Spying her and Cubby making their way toward him, he cast her a resigned smile.

Cubby's hand slipped out of hers and he barreled himself toward Sawyer. Fortunately, his big brother saw him coming and caught him before he plowed right into him. Lifted the boy into his arms.

"We found you!" Cubby grinned in triumph.

"That you did, bud."

Landon punched Cubby's foot. "I found him first."

"Yeah, you did," Sawyer soothed, with a reassuring pat to Landon's shoulder.

"He can sit with us now, can't he, Tori?" Landon turned hope-filled eyes on her. "We have lots of room."

"Of course he's welcome to sit with us, but your brother may not be here to see the play." Her heart still hammering an anxious beat, she gave him a pointed look, hoping he understood her unspoken words. *Is everything okay?*

"Tori's right. I'm here long enough to drop off a check with someone who said he'd be here tonight."

The tension eased. The Selbys were fine. But both boys stared at him, their disappointment evident.

"You're not staying?" Cubby's lower lip protruded, his expression darkening to thundercloud proportions, and she caught alarm flashing through Sawyer's eyes. He no doubt recognized the makings of a public meltdown.

He gave the boy a hug, then set him down on his feet. "This is a little kid's play, buddy. I'm a big kid."

"Tori's a big kid and she made the costumes, too." Landon looked around the now-crowded space, noting mothers, fathers and grandparents in abundance. "There are lots of big kids. Don't you want to sit with us?"

Sawyer glanced uncertainly at Cubby, whose lower lip was trembling. The overhead lights dimmed, then brightened again, signaling that audience members should be seated.

"Sawyer can't stay tonight." She reached for Landon's hand, then stretched out her other one to Cubby. "Let's find our seats. The play is going to start. It'll be fun."

But Cubby shook his head and turned away from her. Standoff.

She sent a pleading look in Sawyer's direction. Surely he could suffer through a single hour with his brothers, couldn't he? Having spent but a week under the same roof with them, she hardly knew the boys, nor they her. She had no "street cred" with them. Hadn't yet gained their respect or established her own authority beyond Ray's warning, as he and Therese departed, to "do what Tori tells you to do."

The lights abruptly dimmed and as her eyes adjusted to the darkness she looked anxiously toward the stage, where Pastor Garrett McCrae stepped out in front of the curtain to welcome everyone.

"I guess I could stay," Sawyer whispered. "Sure won't be able to find my friend now, even if he's here."

Landon squeezed her hand in excitement and, in the dim light, she felt Cubby searching for her other hand. Meltdown avoided. *Thank You, Lord.*

It took a bit of doing, but they found their pew near the front. Landon slipped in first, she followed, then Cubby and Sawyer. But they'd barely gotten situated when Cubby stood again and maneuvered his way to the other side of Sawyer. They all shifted in their limited space, leaving her sitting next to the rugged outdoorsman.

Like she'd be able to pay attention to the play with his rock-solid arm brushing against hers.

Chapter Four

Sawyer wasn't quite sure how he'd gotten himself roped into this, but despite the twins' manipulative tactics and the silently persuasive appeal by the woman now seated next to him, he had a sneaking feeling he was at fault. If he'd paid Kyle what was due him last week or had at least gotten out to his friend's place before dark today, he wouldn't have been lurking in the church doorway, where the boys could spy him.

He glanced at Tori from the corner of his eye, noting her attention was as rapt on the unfolding scenes before them as was that of his brothers. In his own defense, he had no idea she'd be taking the boys out tonight. Where were Therese and Ray anyway? Wasn't it too soon to be leaving Cubby and Landon solely in the care of newly hired help? Sure, she was the help *he'd* recruited. But still...

Even though it lasted only an hour and he hadn't minded in the least sitting by the sweet-smelling young woman next to him, he was restless by the time the youthful actors joined hands across the stage for the final applause. It hadn't been a half-bad production. You know, if you were into that sort of thing. He'd been impressed, too,

by the costumes Tori apparently had a hand in design-
ing. Especially the shiny-scaled dragon that had the kids
roaring each time he muffed well-known Bible verses.
At first Sawyer had worried the actor had forgotten his
lines, but as the play progressed that fear was put to rest.

"You are, aren't you, Sawyer?" Landon tugged on his
sleeve as they stepped into the wide aisle, but Sawyer's
eyes were scanning the packed sanctuary for his friend.
It had been a long, trying day and he'd rather not have to
attempt finding Kyle's place on those unlit back roads.

"Are you?" Cubby echoed.

"What's that?"

"Cookies." Landon clarified. "Are you staying for
cookies?"

"Cookies? No, afraid not."

"But—"

"Boys." Tori's soft voice sounded firm as she drew
their attention. "Your brother did as you asked and stayed
for the play. But he can't stay for cookies, too."

"But we can, can't we?" Cubby's eyes searched hers.

"Yes. You each can have one cookie."

"One?" Landon's mouth dropped open. "Are you kidding me? Sawyer, can't we have more than one?"

He glanced down at Landon, then met the look Tori
leveled at him. "Uh, no. Only one."

She smiled and his heart beat a jerky rhythm. He'd
personally give up sweets altogether if she'd keep smiling at him like that. He again scanned the crowd. If he
could find Kyle, he might give in and join the twins for
postproduction refreshments. *Ah, there he was.*

Pulling the check from his wallet, he quickly made
his way to his friend's side and handed it over.

"Here you go, pal. Sorry again about the delay."

"No problem." Kyle's expression clouded over. "Everything's okay? I mean—"

"Cash flow. Scout's honor." He and Kyle had been friends since they were teenagers working at Hunter's Hideaway for several summers. Then buddies in college. Neither had been Boy Scouts, but he'd get the drift.

Kyle nodded, satisfied, then cocked his head in the direction from which Sawyer had come. "Who's the chick?"

"Chick?"

"The blonde you and the boys were sitting with. I've seen her here before. Seems to be a sweet gal, so I never associated her with the likes of you." He elbowed Sawyer. "Getting back in the game, are you?"

"Don't get any ideas." Would no one who knew him in his college days ever believe he'd turned over a new leaf? "She's a part-time nan—caregiver Therese and Ray Selby hired for my little brothers. Tonight's her first solo evening event with them. Since I was here to see you, I stepped in to help keep the peace."

Now might not be the best time to admit to hiring her to help at the Outpost.

Kyle tucked the check in his shirtfront pocket, then reached for his jacket. "Whatever you say."

But when Sawyer turned back to where he'd left his brothers, they and Tori were gone. Probably off to get their one cookie.

Tori was tougher than she looked.

Much to his own surprise he found himself in the fellowship hall searching her out. The boys were in the refreshment line, Tori farther away, off to one side of those milling about.

"Not into cookies?" he said as he slipped in to stand next to her. "Not even *one*?"

She laughed. "You think I'm a meanie, don't you?"

"I'm not the boss here. That's what you were hired for."

"Well, if you must know, Ray keeps a box of Girl Scout cookies on the kitchen counter and occasionally helps himself to one throughout the day."

"And the boys discovered it and are regularly making off with more than a few themselves."

"Bingo. I had to call them on it. Pointed out that those belong to their grandpa and they hadn't been invited to partake."

He nodded approval. "Even something as minor as that needs to be reined in for the boys' own good. Not only putting a halt to absconding with Ray's personal treats, but limiting the sugar consumption. This is the kind of thing I appreciate you being on top of."

"You still understand, though, don't you, that I'm not your spy in the Selby household?"

"You made that loud and clear."

"I don't want there to be any misunderstanding."

"Not a chance." But was she, by making a point of this again tonight, alluding to the fact that perhaps she'd seen things that concerned her? Things more serious than a potential sugar overload or "grand theft cookie"?

She glanced at her watch. "As soon as the boys finish their punch—and *cookie*—we'd better start for home. If Ray and Therese are back, they'll wonder what happened to us."

"They're out for the evening?" How many other times that he wasn't aware of had they left the kids with a babysitter and gone out on the town?

"There's a visitation at the funeral home in Canyon Springs," Tori continued, "then out to dinner with friends whose family member passed away."

Okay, maybe that was legit.

As they waited for the boys, they chatted about nothing of particular importance—a welcome break in the winter weather, her settling into the apartment and no signs of a mouse.

"Ready to go?" Tori smiled as the boys approached, downing the last bites of what he didn't quite trust had been a single cookie each. "Bundle up and we'll head out. Full moon tonight, so it should be a pretty walk."

Sawyer frowned. "You walked? On a bitterly cold night like this?" Hunter Ridge wasn't that well lit either. Not once you got away from the business district along the main road through town.

She nodded almost guiltily. "I didn't feel comfortable at night driving or trying to park the big SUV that Therese and Ray left for my use. It has car seats for the boys, but they look complicated and by the time I realized that, I knew I'd never figure out how to get them moved to my car in time for the play."

He helped her into her coat. "Let me give you a lift home, then."

Her expression brightened. "You have booster seats?"

"No, but—"

"Then we'll walk."

Stubborn little thing. Yeah, he knew the state laws, but it wasn't *that* far of a drive and it wasn't like he'd be hot-rodding. "Well, then, you won't be walking alone. Come on, boys, get those coats and mittens on."

She lightly touched his arm. "You don't have to do this, Sawyer. We'll be fine."

"I'm sure you will be, but there's no harm in keeping things on the safe side, is there?"

She gave what he took to be a resigned sigh. Too bad. As he held open an exit door to the fellowship hall for

Tori and the boys, his friend Kyle caught his eye and gave him a thumbs-up.

Sawyer let the door slam shut behind him.

Outside, the kids scampered across the dimly lit parking lot, pausing only long enough to skim across frozen puddle patches as Tori attempted unsuccessfully to keep up, her warnings to slow down unheard by squealing four-and-a-half-year-olds.

He shook his head, then let out a piercing whistle that stopped all three in their tracks.

"Put the brakes on it, boys. Slow it down."

Although the twins grumbled, they obeyed, waiting for Tori to catch up and for Sawyer to join them. Then the foursome headed off again, the boys leading the way.

"You'll have to teach me how to whistle like that." Tori's tone held a note of admiration. "I think it may come in handy in this job."

"Easier to buy you a whistle, I imagine."

"Probably."

As they left the parking lot, overhead light diminished considerably despite the rising round-faced moon, and Tori switched on a pocket flashlight.

"You've come prepared."

"I gave ones to the boys, too, if they'd remember to pull them out."

"What's the fun of that when you can run blindly into the dark and fall into a snowbank?"

"True."

They walked in silence for some distance, the voices of the boys, not far ahead, chattering about the nighttime adventure.

"So, how's your first week on duty been?"

"Pretty good. Not a whole lot of time to myself right

now—the boys seem to find their way to my apartment quite frequently."

"I can see how that might be a problem."

"I think once they get used to me being there, I'll be less of a fascination."

He doubted that, but he'd let her think what she wanted to. "If you can find the time next week, you should practice driving the Selbys' bruiser of an SUV in the daylight. You may need it the next time a winter storm system moves through. Depending on where you have to go, that compact of yours might not be able to handle it."

Her chin lifted as if she didn't like to be told what to do.

"At any rate," he continued, not giving her a chance to argue, "you need to tell the Selbys to invest in an extra set of booster seats that you can keep in your car. The boys are big enough that the backless kind should suffice now. Ray and Therese's can probably be converted, too."

They'd run out of sidewalk, had shifted to walk along the edge of the road, and Tori called out a reminder to go single file. At least the snow had melted enough that they didn't have to walk in the roadway itself. The boys had pulled out their flashlights, too, sparring as though with lightsabers.

"Does it seem funny, Sawyer, to have brothers—half brothers—so much younger than you?"

He figured it wasn't anyone's business what he thought of it, since Dad had never asked his opinion on the subject. But he sensed Tori's question was sincere interest, not prying.

"I have two other brothers not too many years older than me. But yeah, it does feel funny at times. I've had people think Cubby and Landon are my kids."

"I can see why. They resemble you. Your dad, he was divorced? Widowed?"

"Widower. When he moved to town to work with me at the Outpost, he met Vanessa Selby—Therese and Ray's youngest daughter—who was fifteen years his junior. She'd spent most of her adult life on a mission field in South America. Never married. No children, but still young enough to have them and—" he chuckled, still marveling at how excited Dad had been when Vanessa announced she was pregnant "—lo and behold, that's exactly what Anderson and Vanessa Banks did."

"How old was your dad when the twins were born?"

"Fifty-three."

"Brave man."

"That's my dad, alright. But after he'd lived alone for so many years, I could hardly begrudge him a little happiness."

"It's a shame it was short-lived."

"Yeah. It is." More than anyone knew.

"There are so many things I can't pretend to understand," she said softly, "and this is one of them."

He didn't understand it either. Oh, he understood the free-will part, that he'd used his to mess up and there had been deadly consequences. But just as when his mother died from a series of strokes when he was eleven, where was God when Dad arrived home to find the house on fire? Where was He when Dad got the boys out, but couldn't save Vanessa, too?

A muscle tightened in his throat. No, he didn't understand it at all.

"I'm sorry if I've stirred sad memories."

She'd picked up on that, had she?

As they approached the Selbys' place and the boys raced ahead, the porch light softly illuminated Tori's face, her compassion-filled eyes. She halted at the edge of the yard. "You lost your father like your little brothers did."

"But I had him for a lot of years," he reminded her quietly. "I have *real* memories of the greatest mom and dad in the world. Memories my younger brothers will never have."

"No, but you can make your memories of him come alive for them, can't you? Teach them about the man their daddy was? You can show them by example the way he lived and how he'd want them to live, too."

That sounded nice, but he *hadn't* lived the way his father had. Not by a long shot.

Before he could respond, an approaching car slowed and turned into the driveway, headlights briefly flashing over them. The Selbys were back, and they probably weren't overjoyed to see him standing in the shadows with Tori.

"Thank you for walking us home, Sawyer."

"Anytime."

As their grandparents exited the vehicle, the boys dashed off the porch and into their open arms.

Sawyer caught Ray's pointed stare in his direction. No doubt the boys' grandfather would be having a heart-to-heart with Tori tonight.

Warning her to keep her distance.

Chapter Five

"The way you talk, you kids must think your mom and dad are ready to be put out to pasture."

At the sound of Therese's brittle laughter, Tori paused in the doorway to the kitchen Thursday morning. She was on the phone, pacing the floor, but motioned Tori to come in. In the two weeks since Tori started the job, she and the boys' grandmother had fallen into taking turns preparing lunch on weekdays. Never anything elaborate or time-consuming. Healthy and light. But it was an enjoyable family time for the five of them. Today was Tori's day as chef.

"Well, stop with the worrying, Curtis," Therese continued as Tori opened a cabinet and pulled out the boys' favorite drinking glasses. Superman for Landon. Snoopy for Cubby. "We're doing fine. Maybe slowing down. But I've read that seventies are the new sixties, you know. We don't need any of you hovering over us…Yes, we now have help with the boys. A nice young woman who attends our church…Yes. Yes. Experienced with kids. She's working out beautifully."

She rolled her eyes at Tori and used her shoulder to tuck the phone by her ear, then opened the fridge to pull out a gallon of milk and set it on the counter. "If something comes up and we need help, trust that we still know how to pick up the phone...What? That's not putting a whole lot of confidence in your dear old mom, now, is it?...Yes. Yes. I love you, too. Talk to you later."

Therese hung up the landline phone. "Kids!"

Tori looked up from where she was setting the table. "Giving you a hard time?"

"Curtis. He's our oldest. All our kids live in Los Angeles now and have been at us to move there, too, ever since we retired from teaching. But we want no part of that." She shook her head. "Curtis has it in his head that Ray and I are on our last legs and don't have the combined sense of a goose. Now he thinks the boys are too much for us. You know, at our *advanced* age."

"Little boys can be a handful."

"We're doing fine with a housekeeper coming in twice a week, and with you here, everything is more than fine." She gave Tori a thankful smile. "So what's for lunch? Is there anything I can do to help, besides pour the milk?"

"I thought we'd have turkey tacos, French green beans, orange slices and ants-on-a-log."

Therese's eyes widened. "Dear me, what's that? Or maybe I don't want to know."

Tori reached into the refrigerator's vegetable bin and pulled out a celery bunch. "Sliced celery ribs filled with crunchy peanut butter and topped with raisin 'ants' arranged like they're crawling on it."

Therese laughed. "Cubby and Landon will love it. Now Ray, that may be a different story."

As it turned out, the ants-on-a-log were a hit with Ray as well as with the twins. Then shortly after lunch Tori headed off to the Outpost, where she'd started the day before yesterday. For the time being, it looked like

Tuesday, Wednesday and Thursday afternoons would be her designated time in the outdoor-gear shop. The boys usually attended a preschool program two of those afternoons each week, and Outpost hours would be added as she further settled into the boys' routines. Sawyer, fortunately, was open to her need for flexibility.

She still hadn't quite pinpointed the underlying feeling that she'd picked up on between the Selbys and Sawyer. But the night Sawyer walked her and the boys home, she'd almost sensed him tensing when the Selbys drove up. And maybe it was her imagination, but it seemed Ray was more concerned about their walking home instead of driving than the situation warranted. In particular, he'd quizzed her as to how Sawyer had gotten involved.

"Hey, Tori!" Diego Santiago called out when she walked in the door of the Echo Ridge Outpost. "Great timing."

"Yeah? What's up?" Slipping off her coat and drinking in the aromas of leather, WD-40 and what she'd come to know as Hoppe's gun cleaner, she approached the dark-haired young man who was straightening items around the cash register. He was probably about her age, maybe a few years younger, an energetic guy whose love for the outdoors made him a perfect match—unlike her—for working at the outdoor-gear store.

"I got a call that my girlfriend locked herself out of her car. I need to dash by her mom's place and pick up the spare key."

"Nasty day to have that happen. You'd better get going."

"Thanks." He headed toward the door, then paused. "You'll be okay, right? I know you don't know anything about fishing and hunting stuff, but it's been a slow day. I won't be gone long. If someone comes in who's looking for something more serious than a pair of gloves, stall him." He flashed a grin. "Or her."

"I'll be fine. Is Sawyer here?"

He looked at his watch and frowned. "Still at lunch, I guess."

"Okay. Get going."

When she'd hung up her coat and stowed her purse in Sawyer's office, she immediately got to work. He'd left her a sketched diagram of where he wanted merchandise moved or displays rearranged. He agreed with her that the store could use some changing up, that certain items had sat too long in the same place year after year, causing customers to overlook them.

An hour passed before the cowbell over the door clanged, signaling someone had entered the shop. She rounded the corner of a display, expecting to see Diego with an excuse on his lips as to what had taken him so long. But instead, she faced a burly ball-capped man who, when he spied her, raised his brows in mild surprise.

"Where's Sawyer?"

"He should be back…any minute." Now, why'd she say that? He might be back momentarily. And he might not. Maybe it was that this guy was big, bearded and looked a little rough around the edges. She wouldn't care for him to think that she'd been left alone indefinitely. Better to think that Sawyer could walk in on them at any time.

The man grimaced. "Unfortunately, I can't wait. Was in town for an earlier meeting and now I need to hit the road. But could you give him something for me?"

"I'd be happy to."

He pulled a few sheets of folded paper out of his jacket pocket. "See that he gets this, will you? And tell him I'll call him later."

"Sure."

She accepted the papers, then his eyes narrowed. "You're new here, aren't you?"

"Brand-new."

"Well, I have to hand it to old Sawyer for trying to drum up business." With a grin he touched the brim of his cap, then was out the door.

With plans to put the papers on Sawyer's desk, she headed to the back of the store. There she gave them a toss from the office doorway, only to have them slide off on the other side of the desk and onto the floor.

"Arrgh." She rolled his leather chair out of the way, then bent to retrieve the scattered papers. But before she again placed them on the desk, bold red wording stamped across one of the pages caught her eye.

Overdue. Second Notice.

"Whatcha got there?"

With a gasp, she clasped the papers to her chest and spun toward the door. Sawyer.

"You scared me to death! I didn't hear the cowbell."

"I came in the back way." His eyes danced at catching her off guard. "No bells."

"Don't do that to me ever again. I lost a dozen years off my life."

"Sorry." But he didn't look sorry. "So what do you have there?"

She glanced down at the papers, then held them out to him. "Some guy stopped by and said to give these to you. I was, you know, putting them on your desk and accidentally knocked them off."

He unfolded one of the sheets. Took a slow breath, then met her curious gaze with a bleak one of his own.

Exactly what he didn't need right now.

"Didn't your mother ever tell you not to accept anything from a stranger? I could have done without this today."

"Bad news?"

"Not good anyway." He flipped through the other pages, then tossed them onto the desk, facedown. "One of the drawbacks of owning your own business."

"The guy said to tell you he'd call you."

"I don't doubt that he will." Like Kyle, he and Graham had hung out at Hunter's Hideaway as teens, mucking out stalls, cleaning rental cabins and busing tables at the inn's restaurant. Then on to college in Flagstaff. It was probably Graham's idea of a joke to stamp *overdue* across the unpaid bill. Or at least he hoped so. "Did he say anything else?"

"No. He wasn't here long. Said he was in town on other business, but couldn't wait until you came back."

"Where's Diego?"

"His girlfriend locked herself out of her car and he went to help."

He nodded, then glanced at the papers on the desk. "You probably saw what Graham gave you to give me, didn't you?"

"I didn't mean to. I—"

He raised a hand as he lowered himself into one of the side chairs. "Don't worry about it. You'll get paid. I always meet my payroll obligations."

"I wasn't worried."

"That's good, because there's no need to be. There have been unanticipated expenses with the store this past year. And despite accruing a cushion for emergency situations, the timing is such that I've gotten into some cash-flow issues. Have to pick and choose who gets paid when."

She nodded. But he doubted she had a clue.

"You'll figure it out. I have confidence in you."

He chuckled. "Nice try, Tori, but you hardly know me. How can you make a statement like that?"

"I can because—" She moved to drop into the upholstered chair beside him, her expression earnest. "Because although I haven't been here long, I've seen firsthand how hard you work. Seen how you love this place. How much you enjoy helping people find the right equipment to get the most out of their outdoor experiences."

"You've seen that, have you?"

"I have. It's been my experience that people with a passion for something always find a way. I know you will, too."

As dumb as it seemed, his heart swelled as her words pumped into him a renewed determination. He *did* have a passion for the Outpost. One that Tori actually recognized. He loved the outdoors and loved providing a variety of means for other people to enjoy it, as well.

He leaned back in his chair to study her thoughtfully. "You know, I think hiring you may be the best thing I've done in a long while."

Their gazes held, then she abruptly broke eye contact and rose to her feet. "Of course it is. Your friend—Graham? He said he has to hand it to you for hiring me to drum up business."

Sawyer let loose a belly laugh. "He did, did he? Well, that old dog may be right."

She shook her head apologetically. "But of course, he didn't know that I don't know the difference between fly-fishing and lure fishing. Or a shotgun from a rifle."

"But you're starting to pick up on the lingo, aren't you?"

"Just enough to be dangerous."

"I think—" he couldn't help but smile at her innocence "—that Graham was making a point that a little thing like that won't much matter when it comes to you making a sale."

She stared at him uncomprehendingly for a long moment, then abruptly her eyes flashed fire. "That's not why you hired me, is it? To be a token female lure of some kind for your stupid store?"

"Now the store—the one you've convinced me I have such great passion about—is stupid?"

"You know what I mean."

"Yes, I know what you mean. And you can calm down. I hired you because I need you to stay in town to take care of my brothers and because—"

Her eyes narrowed. "Because what?"

"Because I do need help getting things in shape. After the excessive expenses on this place, I have to turn things around this year. I can tell that you have a talent for setting up effective displays that puts me to shame. An understanding of balance and color that will catch a customer's eye. And that, Tori, is what will lead to more sales."

"You think so?"

"I wouldn't say it if I didn't mean it. That's one thing you'll learn if you stick around here long enough. I say what I mean and I mean what I say."

He might not have always followed in his father's footsteps, but that was one thing he'd stuck to his guns on.

"I'll do a good job for you, Sawyer." Her eyes took on an intensity, communicating that it was important to her that he believe her. "Even though I'll never be able to answer customer questions or close a sale on much of anything."

Her half smile was weighted with apology.

"Who says you'll never do that? True, maybe not today

or tomorrow, but I'll make an outdoorsman—woman? person?—of you yet."

She shook her hair back with an appealing sassiness. "Fat chance."

He rose to his feet, unable to suppress a grin and feeling more optimistic than he'd felt in months. "Watch me."

"Tori?"

Later that evening, she glanced up from where she was sorting stacks of quilting fabric on top of her bed to see Cubby standing in the doorway. Dressed in Snoopy-themed pajamas, he looked adorable. She'd taken to leaving her door open during the daytime and early evening, even when she wasn't on duty. Somehow it made her feel more a part of the household and it communicated to the boys that they were welcome to come see her at any time.

"Come in, Cubby."

He joined her and reached out to gently pat a blue-and-white-striped square. "I like this one."

"I do, too. That's one of the pieces of material I'm going to use to make a baby quilt. You know, a blanket."

His forehead wrinkled as he looked curiously around the room. "You have a baby?"

"No, no baby. I'm making a quilt to sell to someone who does have a baby."

"I used to be a baby." He looked her in the eye as if reassuring her of the truth of his statement. "But now I'm big."

"Yes, you are. And someday you'll be as big as your big brother."

"Yeah." Cubby's eyes rounded. "He's *real* big."

"He is." Not that she'd noticed that broad chest and the width of his shoulders…

Cubby sidled around the edge of the bed closer to her

as he watched her sort the fabric. "I wish he would come see us again."

"I imagine he will."

"He doesn't come a lot. When we were little, he did."

"He has a business to run and has to work most of the time." A struggling business, in fact. She'd felt his embarrassment when he suspected she'd seen the overdue notice. "But you're special to him."

Cubby shrugged, as if someone thinking you were special held no substance if it wasn't backed up by action.

He ran his hand across a soft flannel fabric, then looked at her with hope-filled eyes. "Would you ask him to come again? Soon?"

"Time for bed, Cub."

They both looked up to see Ray standing in the doorway, a troubled look on his face. How long had he been standing there?

Cubby frowned. "Already? But—"

"No buts. You know the rules, young man."

Landon had confided them to her last week. For every bedtime delay, they had to go to bed ten minutes earlier the following night.

"Okay." He looked at her glumly, Sawyer forgotten. "Good night, Tori."

"Good night, Cubby."

When grandson and grandfather departed, she shut and locked the door, again wondering about Sawyer's relationship with the boys' grandparents. Therese and Ray hadn't said anything about keeping the boys away from Sawyer. Surely they would have if they had true concerns?

She hoped, though, that while she hadn't promised Cubby to ask Sawyer to come again—soon—she hadn't set false expectations in Cubby's mind about Sawyer.

Right now, his big brother had more on his mind than two preschoolers.

When he'd explained that afternoon about his cash-flow situation, she could tell he didn't think she could understand, but she understood better than he assumed. While as a kindergartner she'd not been privy to the details leading up to her parents' divorce, shaky finances had played a part in it—her father's risky investments and, her grandmother later confirmed, the pair's gambling habits.

On down the road there had been a few years of financial instability for her and Grandma, as well. Everything coming due at once. Rent. Car insurance payments. Utilities. Phone bill. Grandma's unexpected medical expenses. They had to prayerfully choose which ones to pay off first, which ones to put down minimal payments.

Not a fun time. So she *did* understand his situation.

Sawyer said she shouldn't worry, that she'd be paid. But even with housing, the part-time wage the Selbys provided wasn't enough to cover more than the most basic of her expenses. Not enough to build a nest egg.

She ran her hand across the soft flannel piece that Cubby had stroked almost lovingly. So while she would do her best not to worry, if she wanted to stay in Hunter Ridge she couldn't afford to miss a single paycheck.

She wanted to be here for the twins. And was more than a little intrigued by their big brother.

Chapter Six

"Are you not feeling well this morning, Therese?"

Tori knelt on the kitchen floor with dampened paper towels Wednesday morning, wiping up the powdered orange drink's gritty granules. The open container had slipped from her employer's hands moments ago, the second time that morning that Tori had observed a mishap.

Therese let out a breathy huff and wet a few more paper towels to hand to her. "I'm fine. That old arthritis acting up."

"If you need any help opening anything, let me know. My grandma had arthritis in her hands, too, so I know how painful that can be."

"Thanks, sweetheart. And thank you for cleaning up this mess—and the other one—so I don't have to get down on these bony old knees."

"What do we have here?" Ray peeked in the kitchen door. "Do we have our fair Cinderella scrubbing the floors now?"

"I dropped something." Therese's tone sounded cross, and Tori glanced up to see her brows lowered at her husband as if in warning. What was that about?

Tori rose and tossed the paper towels in the trash can. "Why don't you let me mix your drink for you?"

"One for me, too, please," Ray added, pulling out a chair for his wife, then seating himself across from her. "You're working at the Outpost today, aren't you, Tori?"

"I'm scheduled to. But Sawyer knew from the get-go that some flexibility would be required to prioritize my responsibilities to you and the boys. Do I need to make a few adjustments today?"

"If you don't mind." He folded his hands on the table in front of him, a determined look in his eyes. "Therese and I need to make a quick trip out of town."

His wife gave him a sharp look. "There's no need to disrupt Tori's day. Or Sawyer's either. Whatever it is you have in mind can wait."

His chin jutted. "Maybe it can't."

"I'm more than happy to change my schedule." Tori looked from one to the other. "Say the word and I'll give Sawyer a call." It wasn't like she was waiting on customers. He wouldn't be left in the lurch in that respect.

Both spoke at once. Ray with a grateful *thanks* and Therese with an uncompromising *no, thank you.*

Okay. Tori placed the drinks on the table in front of them just as the boys burst into the room, Landon scrambling into a chair next to his grandpa.

"May I have a sip, G'ma?" Cubby stood respectfully by Therese's side, not making a grab for her drink as some kids Tori had worked with would have been inclined to do.

"You may." Therese smiled as she reached for the glass. But she only succeeded in tipping it over, sending it rolling and the orange liquid gushing across the blue-and-white-checked tablecloth.

Landon and Cubby both yelped, but a quick-thinking

Ray rose and snatched the glass before it rolled off the edge and shattered on the floor. His concerned gaze zeroed in on Therese, whose head was lowered.

Then she looked up, the usual spark in her eyes subdued. "I'm sorry, Tori. I've made another mess for you to clean up."

"Don't worry about it."

Ray helped his wife from her chair. "Maybe you should rest before we go."

Landon homed in on that comment. "Where are you going, Grandpa?"

"Crazy," Ray shot back with a grin as Therese pulled away without argument and left the room. "Want to go?"

The boys laughed, waving him off. Ray nodded to Tori, his voice lowering as he stepped closer. "If you can make arrangements with Sawyer, it would be appreciated."

"I will. No problem. But...is Therese okay?"

He offered a reassuring smile. "You know that old Arthur-Itis. Frustrates her to no end. But her meds may need some adjustment, then she'll be as right as rain."

He smiled at the boys, then followed in the direction Therese had taken.

Under the watchful eyes of the twins, Tori quickly removed the stained tablecloth and took it to the laundry room to soak. Grandma Eriksen's arthritis had become increasingly problematic in the damper summer days when monsoons rolled across the state. Here in the high elevations, Therese not only had to cope with summer rains, but winter cold and dampness, as well.

"Can I drink Grandpa's juice?" Landon peered over the countertop where she'd placed it.

"Yes, please do. And I'll mix some up for you, too, Cubby."

Both boys pulled out a chair and sat down, Cubby exchanging a knowing look with his brother. "G'ma drops a lot of things, doesn't she?"

Landon nodded. So this wasn't the first time the kids had noticed.

"That's because her hands are stiff," she explained. "They hurt. It's hard to hold on tight."

"Is that why she takes naps, too?"

"Maybe." Tori hadn't been aware of Therese taking naps, but then lots of adults took naps. "Power naps," some called them.

She mixed up Cubby's juice, then sliced a banana and started the oatmeal while the boys discussed the latest thing in kids' toys that they'd seen on TV. She'd just set their breakfasts in front of them when the phone on the wall rang.

Landon leaped from his chair. "I'll get it."

He'd whipped the phone out of its cradle before the second ring.

"Selbys. Hello?" He nodded at whatever the speaker had said, then held out the receiver to her. "It's for you. Sawyer."

Why had he called her here and not her cell? He must have tried her number and she hadn't heard it from where she'd left it in the apartment. "Good morning, Sawyer."

"Hey, Tori. I was wondering…any chance you could come in earlier today? FedEx made a delivery and I could use some help getting it inventoried and readied for display."

"Actually, I was about to call you. Something's come up and I won't be in today."

"Are the kids okay?"

"They're fine." But she didn't think the Selbys would appreciate her sharing personal information. Therese's health appeared to be a sensitive issue, one that seemed to embarrass her. "Ray and Therese have business to take care of out of town and asked if I'd rearrange my schedule to be here for the boys all day."

He was silent a moment. "Why not bring them with you?"

"Do you think that's a good idea?" She glanced toward the table, where Landon was flying his spoon rather aggressively in Cubby's direction. Two active boys and a shop loaded with fishhooks, hunting knives and guns seemed like misadventure waiting to happen.

"Dad used to bring them here. You know, when Vanessa had other things going on. We didn't have any problems."

"I guess that would be alright." Should she run it by Ray and Therese first, or would that give them something needless to worry about? "You know, if you're sure."

"I'm sure. They need to be around stuff like this anyway. Dad had big plans to make them outdoorsmen. Fishermen, hikers and campers."

Sawyer sounded almost excited at the prospect of her bringing them with her. Maybe this was an opportunity for him to begin sharing common interests. Brotherly bonding. Time spent together without Therese and Ray looking over his shoulder. While unboxing merchandise and entering inventory into the computer, she could keep a close eye on them. Maybe they could even help her.

"Okay, then. We'll see you soon."

"And this," Sawyer said from where he squatted in front of the boys, noting their rapt attention as he held out a flat circular device in his open palm, "is a compass. It helps you get your bearings when you need to know which direction to go."

"That pointy thing keeps moving," Cubby observed, as Sawyer turned his hand slightly.

"It will always point northward."

"Like at the North Pole."

"The opposite direction will always be south. And," he said, pointing, "if this is north and that is south, then these two would be east and west."

"The sun rises in the east." Landon bobbed his head knowingly. "And sets in the west."

"That's right."

Cubby leaned in for a closer look. "Where did you get this thing?"

"It used to belong to our grandpa. Our dad's dad."

Cubby's eyes widened. "Wow. It's old."

Sawyer chuckled as he glanced at Tori, who sat across the room in the middle of a stack of boxes. He caught her amused smile. "Yeah, I guess it is old."

"It's funny, isn't it," Landon said, his forehead creased thoughtfully as he studied Sawyer, "that we have the same daddy? I mean, you look *old.* Like some of my friends' dads. But you're our brother."

Sawyer smothered a smile and didn't need to look in Tori's direction to confirm she'd be laughing. "I guess it is kinda funny. And don't forget, you have two other half brothers, as well. My big brothers."

"I don't remember them." Cubby's face scrunched. "Maybe a little."

Brandon and Thomas had come for the funeral, and the kids may have seen them at the house. But both lived out of state and, having grown up in metro Phoenix, couldn't understand their dad's and youngest brother's fascination with a dinky town like Hunter Ridge. Would his little brothers develop a love for Arizona's backcountry as Dad had hoped, or hightail it on out of here after high school graduation and consider themselves well rid of the place?

He'd given some thought to what Tori said earlier about sharing common interests with them. He still had well over a decade to do his part to win them over on Dad's behalf. He might not be the world's greatest example in some areas of his life, but he did know and love the outdoors.

Handing the compass to Cubby, who cradled it reverently in his small hands, Sawyer stood to extract his wallet from his back pocket, then squatted again to pull a photo from it. "Recognize anybody?"

The boys crowded around.

"That's Grandpa Banks, Dad's dad." He pointed to the oldest man in the picture, who knelt in front of a tent, towering ponderosa pines in the background. "Then our dad's the one in the baseball cap. And that's me with my backpack. I was thirteen."

The photo had been taken a few years after his mother died. Grandpa, it seemed, had noticed his only son was floundering, directionless, and his youngest grandson had given up his own interests to keep his widower father company. So he decided to step in. That was the first of many outdoor adventures that Sawyer enjoyed throughout his teen years.

"Mommy and Daddy took us camping," Cubby chimed in.

"No." Landon shook his head. "That was a picnic."

"Uh-uh. We had a tent, 'member?"

"He did take you on some day-camping trips," Sawyer recalled. "Just not overnighters." He wouldn't mention to the boys that their dad and mom had been making plans for that come springtime. They'd bought a new sleeping bag for each and some other gear for pint-size fellows, later tossed out due to smoke damage.

Cubby looked at him wistfully, still carefully guarding the compass in his hands. "I wish you would take us camping."

"Yeah," Landon echoed. "That would be cool."

Sawyer glanced in Tori's direction. She wasn't looking at him, but no doubt was listening in, waiting to hear how he'd respond. He hadn't done overnight camping at such a young age himself, but he had lots of friends who'd taken their diaper-clad kids along, hauling them around in carriers on their backs.

"Maybe…" He wouldn't make any promises. He'd have to get Therese and Ray's approval first. "Maybe I could take you camping. You know, someday."

But the boys didn't hear the "someday" disclaimer.

"Oh, man!" Landon fist pumped the air, and Cubby let out a piercing squeal.

You'd have thought he'd told them to pack up their gear and meet him at the pickup in five.

"Woo-hoo!" Cubby, too often solemn, grinned from ear to ear. "Can Tori go, too?"

Caught off guard at their enthusiasm, he motioned them to quiet down. "Hold your horses, guys. This isn't something we can do right away. I imagine your grandma and grandpa Selby will need to think about it and probably ask us to wait until it's warmer."

"Awww." Landon's former smile dipped downward.

Cubby sighed. "G'ma and G'pa will never let us go."

"Why do you say that?" Tori had left her inventorying and approached to join them.

Cubby looked up at her. "'Cause G'ma doesn't like bugs."

"Or dirt," Landon added. "Or boys dragging it in the house on their shoes."

"Your grandma doesn't have to go if she doesn't want to." She made it sound as if this was a done deal, but he wasn't naive enough to think Ray and Therese wouldn't voice objections. "So I say we wait and see how they feel about it."

A now-smiling Landon elbowed his brother, and Cubby giggled.

"Remember, too," Sawyer added, "that you have lots to learn and gear to pull together before you can think about going on an overnight camping trip."

The boys turned eagerly to him again.

"You'll need backpacks and water bottles. Sleeping bags." He had that stuff here at the Outpost and had often helped customers outfit their youngsters. Sunscreen. Pint-size sunglasses. Brimmed hats.

"A compass?" Cubby asked hopefully, carefully handing his grandfather's back to Sawyer.

"Yes, compasses. And whistles."

Landon looked skeptical. "Whistles?"

"In case of an emergency or if you'd get lost."

"I won't get lost." Landon squared his shoulders and cast his brother a challenging look.

Cubby puffed out his own chest. "Me neither."

"Well, that's good to know, but there are things we have to do before we can think of taking an overnight camping trip." Not the least of which was winning over Therese and Ray, who—although they'd never said so right to his face—he had a sneaking suspicion didn't approve of him.

And for good reason, even if they didn't know the whole of it.

"So let's not mention it to your grandma and grandpa just yet, okay? Not until I can talk to them."

Expecting Tori might object, he was pleasantly surprised when the look and slight nod she gave him conveyed she agreed that would be a wise move. He didn't quite know what to think of it, this newly acquired habit he was falling into of hoping to please Tori Janner...

Chapter Seven

"Tori?" Ray stood in the doorway of her apartment that evening. "May I speak with you a moment?"

She looked up from her sewing machine. "Sure."

He motioned for her to follow him, and she locked the door behind her as she always did to keep the boys safely out of her sewing supplies. Needles and pins. Scissors.

"Therese seemed more herself tonight," she commented as they walked down the hallway and past the sweeping staircase. "Although tired."

"Yes, definitely tired." They entered the high-ceilinged parlor. Ray sat down on an upholstered love seat, motioning her to a nearby chair. "Make yourself comfortable. This won't take long."

Make herself comfortable? Amid the antiques, velvets and brocades? Old sepia-toned photographs and fragile bric-a-brac added to the air of formality. An unhappy little boy hadn't scared her off from the job offer, but this room in which she'd interviewed had come close. No doubt it fueled their big brother's concerns about the active boys growing up here.

"Therese retired for the evening shortly after we ate." Ray stretched an arm across the back of the love seat.

"So I put the boys to bed tonight. Cubby was distraught about something that happened today, which is what I want to talk to you about."

Her mind raced over the events of the day. The laughter. The brotherly bonding. What could have upset him? Nothing that she could think of unless the boys had piped up, despite Sawyer's admonition, and begged to go camping. Then Ray had squashed the idea.

"Now before I continue—" his expression, to her relief, was kind "—I don't seriously mind that you took the boys to work at the Outpost with you today. I threw off your schedule at the last minute."

With a sinking feeling, she nodded. "But something upset Cubby?"

"He cried tonight as I tucked him in."

"Because you said no."

A crease formed between Ray's brows. "Because I said no to what?"

"The boys…" She thought fast. "They're always dreaming things up they want to do. I'm sure you've often had to say no."

"Well, this time the tears were due to grief, not disappointment. Cubby's missing his mother and father, and it seems this episode was triggered by Sawyer talking to them about their dad today. Stirring up memories. Showing them photos."

Her heart wilted. "Honestly, Ray, I was there the entire time and there was no indication from either of the boys that learning more about their parents, particularly their dad, in any way affected them negatively. They seemed quite interested. Asking questions. Not a hint of upset."

"Cubby harbors things deep down. You no doubt recall the meltdown at the ice cream shop?"

"If you don't mind me asking," Tori said, her heart aching for the boy, "what triggered that?"

Ray ran a hand wearily across his eyes. "He was tired. We'd had a busy day. The twins are very different, you know. Temperament. Personality."

She nodded.

"Anyway, he tends to be more of a Gloomy Gus." Ray chuckled. "But what set it off is that we were looking at the menu when Cubby spied a woman out the window who he thought was his mother."

"Oh, no."

"He was excited and pressing himself up against the window, tapping on it and trying to get her attention." Ray shook his head. "Before I knew it, he was halfway to the door. He was steaming mad at me, but I got him back in his seat, explaining that the woman resembled his mother but she was someone else. That his mommy is in Heaven. But he wouldn't hear any of it. And that's when you walked in."

"A sad situation. And he was upset like that tonight?"

"Not to that extreme, thankfully. But nevertheless, his grief was renewed. When I questioned him, he talked about how his mom and dad had taken him and Landon hiking and on picnics. It appears he's troubled by the memories."

"I'm sorry, Ray. Neither Sawyer nor I picked up on that. In fact, I feel responsible because it probably was at my urging that Sawyer mentioned their father at all."

"What do you mean?"

"I thought it might be comforting to the boys to get to know the man their father was through memories Sawyer can share with them. I thought it might help Sawyer, too. He lost the same father the twins did."

"I know you had good intentions, Tori, but—" He

shook his head. "Cubby is an especially sensitive soul. Quick to shed a tear."

"Is that such a bad thing?" She wasn't sure how the words now poised on the tip of her tongue might be taken, but she felt compelled to voice them. "I remember at the ice cream shop you told him that big boys don't cry. There's nothing inherently wrong with a boy crying, especially one who had his parents torn from his life."

Ray snorted. "Unfortunately, we've had way too many tears around here. The boys—particularly Cubby—have discovered waterworks are especially useful in manipulating their grandma."

"But tears," Tori prodded, her heart heavy, "aren't as useful when it comes to swaying Grandpa?"

"I see right through them."

"You know, though, Ray, children need to grieve. Just like adults." Her thoughts again flashed to the memory of her father angrily trying to stop her from crying. "It's healthy for the boys to work through their loss. They need the freedom to talk about their mother and father openly. To share memories with each other and with you. Do you and Therese allow them to do that?"

Ray, looking uncomfortable, stood. "Memories make them sad. I love those two whippersnappers, and I don't like to see them hurting. And while I won't go as far as to forbid you from taking them to the Outpost when necessary, please do me a favor. Ask Sawyer not to talk about his father in the presence of my grandsons."

Two days later, Sawyer glanced over at Tori seated in the front of his pickup. "Do you mind if we swing by my place on the way into Hunter Ridge? I need to pick up something I forgot this morning and it will save me from having to backtrack after I drop you off."

A check needed to be postmarked today to avoid a late penalty.

"I don't mind. I'm curious to see where your place is."

She was? He hoped she wouldn't be disappointed. It wasn't a showplace cabin like some in the region. But from what he'd gleaned during the drive to and from Show Low, she enjoyed Arizona history. His place might interest her as more than just a roof over his head.

They'd had a busy day. With measurements in hand, she'd accompanied him to a business liquidation sale in Show Low and helped him select shelving for the storage room as well as two wood-framed, glass-fronted display cases. He'd go back for them tomorrow with a borrowed Hunter's Hideaway stock trailer.

"My place is nothing fancy," he added, picking up where the conversation had left off. "But it's a genuine old-time cabin that used to serve as a store and post office in Hunter Ridge's earliest years, before the main business district shifted higher up on the forested mesa."

He slowed to turn off the main highway, then they headed down a steep, winding incline that bottomed out at the bridge crossing Hunter's Creek. As they made their way back up the other side, just short of the city limits, he turned onto a narrow gravel road, its curving length lined with oaks and ponderosa pines.

"It's a historic site? But your family isn't originally from around here, is it?"

"No. We've been mostly urban desert dwellers for several generations, but some of us—Grandpa, Dad, me—eventually gravitated to the high country. This place was going to ruin, slated to be torn down, but when I was a teenager my grandpa saw its potential and snatched it up about the same time he bought the Outpost. We'd started renovating it on weekends and holidays and when he passed away not long after I graduated from college, I took over the Outpost and continued work on the cabin."

She nodded with interest as they bumped along the road.

"You know, Tori, I've been giving more thought to that camping trip the boys want to go on." He glanced at her, expecting to see interest in her eyes, but she'd turned to stare out the passenger-side window. Come to think of it, she'd been unusually quiet today, as though something were weighing on her mind. "I was thinking of taking them to one of dad's favorite spots. Great views. Good fishing. Lots of wildlife. Think they'd like that?"

"Probably."

Probably? Not the enthusiastic response he'd come to expect of her. When the boys had first presented the idea, she'd thought it would be a wonderful experience. If the Selbys agreed to the trip, of course.

"The kids haven't said anything to their grandparents about camping yet, have they? You know, before I've decided how best to approach them?"

"Not that I'm aware of."

He glanced at her again as he skirted the truck around a pothole. "You know you're welcome to come along, too, don't you? The boys would love it. And if you'd feel more comfortable, I'll ask Luke and Delaney to join us, or maybe Grady and Sunshine. Their Tessa isn't that much older than the twins, is she?"

"Just a year. Kindergartner."

Was she considering going? Or had his teasing about turning her into an outdoorsman created some anxiety? Maybe she feared he might ask her to bait a fishhook or skin a critter or something.

"You know, though, Sawyer, it might be—"

"There it is." He pointed ahead as through the trees he

spied his two-story tin-roofed cabin's wide front porch. As always at the sight of it, a sense of coming home rose up within him. The location, although feeling remote, was actually not far from civilization, a reasonably walkable distance from town if you didn't mind hoofing it through some rough terrain.

Tori leaned forward. "I love it, Sawyer! It's so cute."

He grinned. Now, *that* reaction was all Tori.

He had to admit, with sunlight dappling down through the pines, it looked as if it had nestled there forever, anchored by a solid stone foundation and logs aged a soft brownish gray. This wasn't a modern "kit" cabin as she'd probably seen in those log home magazines at the grocery store. No, this was the real deal. Around a hundred years old. Slightly behind the main structure was a separate work shed he'd hauled in from another location and a double carport that was later attached.

He pulled to the side of the lane, jumped out to open a steel gate, then drove through. "I'll only be a minute, but do you want to come in?"

"Do dogs bark?" She laughed as two of them dashed around the far corner of the cabin doing just that.

Sawyer climbed out of the truck and the two canines immediately silenced and sat, tails wagging, awaiting permission to move forward to greet him. He rounded the truck and opened the passenger-side door. "It's okay. You can get out. These guys won't jump on you."

She came to stand by him, looking apprehensive at the size of his furry family members. One, a black, white and brown mix, bore traces of an Australian shepherd bloodline and something obviously larger. The other, black as coal, was mostly Labrador.

"Tori, meet Blackie." He pointed at the Lab mix.

She made a face at him. "Now, *that's* an original name."

He laughed as he indicated the mottled one. "And this is Louie."

"Hi, boys." She knelt, and Sawyer signaled to the dogs, who quietly approached, tails wagging, for her to pet. "What sweethearts."

"Hear that, guys? Your fearless leader lives in a *cute* cabin and his dogs are *sweet*. Go figure." He squatted to rough up Louie's neck fur.

Without any urging, Tori followed him up the porch steps and into the house. What would she think of it?

No, she didn't mind a slight detour.

Inside, as Sawyer disappeared down a hall and she heard his footfalls heading up a staircase, she looked eagerly around the open space. There was something appealing about a cabin, especially one that had history tied to the region. His was as cozy as a hobbit home with all the expected trappings of a male domain. Natural stone fireplace. Recliner. Wide-screen TV.

In front of glassed French doors that were no doubt a recent addition, a large oak table with mismatched wooden chairs graced an oval woven rag rug. To the right was a kitchen, lending a modern element to the structure, although its cabinetry appeared to be weathered wood. Did Sawyer cook much? Or was he one of those masters of the frozen microwave meal?

She eased down onto one of the woven-seated stools at the counter that separated the kitchen from the rest of the downstairs space. She'd enjoyed their trip today, with Sawyer entertaining her with tales of working at Hunter's Hideaway as a teen. In turn, she'd related her hopes of establishing a business similar to the one she'd shared with her grandmother in Jerome.

She didn't, of course, include anything about the contributing role that Heath had played in dismantling that enterprise. To her relief, Sawyer genuinely seemed to take her quilting aspirations seriously, not condescendingly as her former fiancé had done. But despite the easy back-and-forth nature of their conversation today, she hadn't relaxed. Not for a minute.

Throughout the trip she'd searched for the courage to slip in Ray's request that Sawyer refrain from discussing his father with his little brothers. She was responsible for planting that idea in Sawyer's mind, and now she had to tell him it was a *bad* idea?

Frustrated, she glanced down at a square, flat-bottomed basket sitting on the counter, crammed with odds and ends of junk mail. Idly, she reached for a colorful fast-food flier and unfolded it. Coupons for burgers and fries. She smiled. They'd expired in December. At least the next ad she pulled out for an oil change and car wash had another week to go on it.

Yes, she needed to tell Sawyer what had happened, but he'd feel hurt—and probably angry—at Ray's directive, and also concerned that he'd caused Cubby distress. What if Sawyer saw the twins before she told him and unknowingly said something that again disturbed one of his little siblings? That wouldn't be fair to any of the Banks brothers.

She pulled a few more fliers from the stack. Flashy-looking ads for well-known Vegas casinos. Special deals on rooms, dining, shopping and shows, offers made in hopes poor suckers—like her dad and mom—would settle in at a slot machine or poker table and empty their pockets. Or savings account.

Shaking her head, she tossed the fliers back into the pile just as Sawyer reappeared, carrying what seemed to be two small photo albums.

"So what do you think of the place?"

"It's fabulous. I don't know what it looked like before, but it's amazing."

"It was in sad shape. Big sections of the roof caved in, broken windows, rotting floors. Ancient wiring and no plumbing."

"As in no…?"

"No running water or indoor bathroom. But now, I'm pleased to say, there are one and a half bathrooms."

She laughed. "Bravo."

He filled her in on the decision to renovate rather than restore so modern conveniences could be incorporated. She could tell he was proud of the place, pleased with how it was turning out.

She nodded to the items in his hands. "Are those pictures of the renovation?"

"Actually—no." He handed her one of the albums.

Puzzled, she opened the gray padded cover of the first book, her heart jolting at a reprint of the same photo Sawyer carried in his wallet and had shown his brothers. As she slowly paged through the album, one photo at a time, each tugged at her heart. Picture after picture of him with his older brothers, grandfather and father enjoying outdoor adventures.

"I thought they'd like having pictures of when their dad was a kid. And their Banks grandparents. And of me, too, you know, when I was their age, doing stuff with Dad. I slipped in some pictures of them with their folks at the back."

She glanced at the burgundy album still in his hands.

"They're identical," he said, catching her look. "Do you think they'll like them?"

She drew a shaky breath. "They will love them. This is truly special, Sawyer."

His eyes brightened at her words. But how could she tell him that right now might not be a good time to share these memories with the boys?

"Sawyer—"

At the blast of a vehicle's horn she startled. Frowning, Sawyer placed the photo albums on the counter, then she followed him to the door. Luke Hunter's crew-cab pickup was pulling into the drive with a slatted stock trailer hitched on behind.

Luke braked and rolled down the truck window. "Where do you want this? Grady said you needed to borrow it for a run to Show Low."

Sawyer stepped off the porch. "Talk about at-your-door service. I called him before we left there and said I could pick it up tomorrow. I didn't expect home delivery."

"No problem. Let me get this thing turned around and help you get it hitched up to that pickup of yours."

"I need to run Tori back into town first."

Luke glanced to where she stood in the cabin's doorway, apparently noticing her for the first time. He raised a hand in greeting, his expression thoughtful. "I can drop her off wherever she needs to go. Save you a trip."

Sawyer looked to her. "Is that okay with you?"

"That's fine."

She retrieved her belongings from Sawyer's truck, then watched from the porch as Luke expertly maneuvered his rig in the small clearing. They unhitched the trailer, then Sawyer positioned his own vehicle and they rehitched it.

With Tori aboard, Luke started his truck slowly toward the gate, but Sawyer flagged them down and jogged up to her window. He pulled a folded envelope from his shirt pocket and handed it to her.

"Do me a favor, will you, please? Drop this off at the post office when you get to town?"

"Sure." She slipped it into her jacket pocket.

But as nice as it was of Luke to give her a ride, she'd lost the opportunity for a heart-to-heart with Sawyer about Ray nixing a sensitive topic of conversation.

The Banks boys' dad.

Chapter Eight

Sawyer woke up Saturday morning knowing that after he claimed his sale items in Show Low, today was the day to broach the subject of camping with the Selbys before one of his brothers let word of it slip. Seeing how excited the twins had been earlier in the week, the idea had been planted in his head and wouldn't let him go.

With his out-of-town chore now completed and the stock trailer returned to Hunter's Hideaway, he headed in the direction of the Selbys' place, feeling almost like a kid himself at the prospect of introducing his brothers to the outdoor world he knew his dad had intended for them to be a part of. And while he was selling the Selbys on the idea, he'd drop off the photo albums for Cubby and Landon, too. Maybe they could spend time going through them together so he could explain who everyone was and the stories behind each photo.

He glanced at the two decorative bags sitting on the seat of his truck. He hadn't been mistaken that Tori had been touched when he'd shown the albums to her.

He had her to thank for getting him over the hurdle of avoiding the boys in order to steer clear of the Selbys, and for making him recognize that he'd been wrong to do that. His dad had encouraged him to be involved in their lives and would have expected him to play an active role now, too. But out of guilt—and fear—he'd backed away.

No more.

Maybe when he finished visiting with Ray and Therese he could start making concrete plans for the camping trip. Sure, they might want to think about it and get back to him. But he'd play up the possibility that Tori and a few other adults with kids would be there. The twins would be well supervised. What more could they ask, except maybe to come along, too?

His spirits rising, he whistled an upbeat tune all the way to the Victorian-style house, where he pulled up on the street out front, behind Tori's blue Kia. Had she followed his advice and spoken to Ray and Therese about extra booster seats? Taken any practice drives in their big SUV?

He snagged the two bags off the seat, then headed up the gravel driveway. He hadn't called ahead, wanting it to appear he was just dropping off the photo albums, then casually following up with "and while I'm here, Ray, I was wondering…" In his mind, he'd gone over a hundred reasons why camping would be a good experience for the boys. Now if only he could present the top ones well.

He was almost to the door when it suddenly opened and a jacketed Tori, purse slung over her shoulder, stepped out on the porch, a surprised look on her face to see him standing there.

"Hey, Tori. How's it going?"

"Good. What brings you here?"

He lifted the bags. "Thought I'd drop off the photo albums. Are Ray and Therese home? I want to talk to them about the camping trip, as well."

She pulled the door closed behind her, voice lowered. "Actually...this isn't a good time."

His spirits faltered. "When do you think would be?"

She caught him by surprise when she stepped forward to loop her arm through one of his and turned him away from the door. "Do you have a minute, Sawyer? To speak in private?"

"I guess so." Confused, he nevertheless let her lead him down the porch steps and back to the street where he'd parked. There she released his arm and stepped away.

"What's up?"

She glanced uneasily toward the house. "I've been meaning to tell you something that Ray shared the day the kids came to the Outpost with me, but there never seemed to be a good time."

Sawyer tensed. She'd spent nearly all day with him yesterday and hadn't found a "good time"? "It can't wait until I give these to Cubby and Landon?"

She glanced at the bags in his hand and shook her head.

"Why not?"

She turned her back to the house. "You can't give them to the boys. Not right now."

"Why not?"

"Ray told me...told me he doesn't want you talking to the boys about your dad—their dad—anymore."

"What?"

"Don't be upset. This is my fault. I'm the one who suggested you share more of yourself, more about your dad, with your brothers."

"And Ray told you that's not a good idea? What kind of crazy talk—"

She touched his arm. "He's concerned."

"About what?"

"When I took the twins to the Outpost with me, Cubby found that upsetting. You know, the talk about his dad."

Sawyer frowned, casting back through memories of the day. "Cubby wasn't upset."

"I didn't think so either. I told Ray that, too. But he said at bedtime Cubby was crying and missing his daddy and, well, Ray tracked it back to the conversations that day. He doesn't want it to happen again."

"Cubby and Landon were all over the picture in my wallet. Openly asked questions. Seemed eager to hear more."

"I know. I was there, remember?"

"So what's the deal not wanting me to talk to the boys about Dad?"

"Personally, Sawyer, I don't think it's all about Cubby. I could be speaking out of turn but I think it's more—" She stopped herself, an almost guilty flicker sparking in her eyes as she glanced away.

"More what?"

"It's just that…" Why did he get the feeling that the long pause was so she could make something up? That she wasn't coming clean? "Ray doesn't like to see Cubby sad. Crying."

"Tori, the kid's mom and dad died. Now he's living in a big scary house with grandparents he didn't know well before that. Therese and Ray love the boys. Don't get me wrong. But they weren't around much before they took the boys in. Always on the go. Don't you think tears might be the norm in a case like that?"

Her hand tightened on his arm. "I agree. And I'm sorry if this news has hurt you. Upsetting the boys wasn't your intention in sharing family stories with them."

Sawyer shook his head. "But now Ray holds me responsible because he thinks I made Cubby cry. Bottom line, he's saying he doesn't want me around because I'll provoke memories that might distress the twins."

"He didn't say that. In fact, he said he had no problems with it if I needed to take the boys to the Outpost with me again." Her eyes appealed for his understanding. "Don't forget, he's grieving, too. And trying to help his grandsons deal with their loss. Doing his best. Please don't be angry with him."

"It's hard not to be, don't you think?" Cutting off the boys from their past, from memories of those who loved them, wasn't the route to go. Could he help it if that made him mad? Mad at himself, too, for lurking in the shadows of the boys' lives for too long. Had he asserted himself right from the beginning, made sure the Selbys knew he intended to play an active role in his siblings' lives, maybe things would be different now.

"I understand, Sawyer, I do."

He lifted the bags in his hand. "So you don't think this is a good idea."

"You put an amazing amount of thought, work and love into those photo albums. The boys will treasure them." She pressed her lips together, her expressive eyes almost pleading. "But…just not right now."

"Then when?"

Tori could hear the hurt in his tone. See it in his troubled eyes. If only she hadn't encouraged him, before she'd settled into the new household, to become more engaged in the lives of his brothers. She'd prematurely pushed him into possible conflict with Ray and Therese before she fully comprehended the dynamics of the varied relationships involved.

Dynamics she still hadn't grasped.

"Just give it a little more time."

"How much?"

To her dismay, the day after Cubby's tearful bedtime she'd noticed a photo of the boys' parents had been moved from the nightstand to a higher-up dresser top. Present, but less visible. And when she'd asked why the twins had been moved to separate rooms, Therese indicated they'd been excited to have their own space. They *did* seem enthused with the idea, maybe Landon more so than Cubby.

But wouldn't sharing a room be a comfort and an opportunity to relive memories? She'd always dreamed of having a sister to confide in. But at least Grandma had been open to her talking about and asking questions regarding her mother and father and didn't shut her down. She'd been honest yet compassionate about the strengths and weaknesses of her daughter and son-in-law.

But how much of the inner workings of the Selbys' personal lives was she at liberty to share with Sawyer? It wasn't as if the boys' lives were in danger.

"I'd wait long enough for Cubby to further adjust. In my opinion, your sharing with him about your dad that day was a good thing, helping him work through his loss. An opportunity to release more tears and get in touch with his feelings."

"But…?"

"But maybe a bit at a time. Not too much that it might be overwhelming."

"Then you probably don't think now is a good time either, to talk to the Selbys about the camping trip the boys seem keen on."

"It may be premature." Would Ray turn him down, thinking conversation regarding the boys' parents was bound to come up? She didn't want a denial added to whatever she sensed might stand between Sawyer and the Selbys. But she knew after listening to his plans yesterday that the idea had taken root in his heart. And now here she was, crushing his hopes.

He glanced toward the house. "I guess I can wait."

Relief flooded through her.

"But I have to say," he added with a grimace, "that it's tempting to drop the photos off and let Ray deal with the repercussions."

"But the boys—"

He held up his hand. "The only reason I'm *not* going to do that is because of the boys. So give me some credit."

"I give you lots of credit, Sawyer. Make no mistake about that."

He looked startled for a fleeting moment, then offered a grim smile. "Well, don't give me *too* much."

"Why not? You're trying to find your way in an uncharted world that includes your brothers and their grandparents. Trying to figure out how you can fit in without stepping on Ray's and Therese's toes. I believe in giving credit where credit is due."

He didn't look convinced, his eyes narrowing. "I wish I hadn't held back so long. That I'd gotten involved in their lives right from the beginning. You know…after their folks died."

"Why didn't you?"

He stiffened. "It was…awkward."

"You've mentioned that before. Surely it couldn't have been any more awkward a year ago than it is now." He'd earlier mentioned how neither he nor the Selbys had known how to fit him in. But how much easier it would have been to have worked through those uncomfortable feelings then rather than now, after time had further set the dynamics and routines of their relationship in stone. But that's what Sawyer seemed to be belatedly recognizing now, as well. Her blunt question and subsequent comment had been out of place. She softened her tone, her gaze now meant to reassure. "No matter how much any of us may want to, we can't go back in time for a do-over, right?"

"Exactly." He glanced again toward the house. "I guess, then, that I'd better get going, seeing as how my whole purpose was to deliver the photos and get camping trip approvals."

"I'm sorry, Sawyer. I didn't mean to ruin your day."

Thankfully, though, she'd happened to be leaving on an errand just as Sawyer arrived. Close call. And one for which she had only herself to blame, having been unable to garner the courage to broach the subject at earlier opportunities.

"The day's not ruined. It's just a little disappointing. I'm glad you let me know, though, before I barged in there not knowing about Cubby's upset and Ray's mandate."

"It's a temporary delay on the camping." She hoped it was anyway. "I'm praying."

He didn't dispute her, but she didn't miss the doubt that flashed through his eyes.

"It's still on the cold side anyway," he continued. "The weather's too iffy to take them camping right now."

"You can still make behind-the-scenes plans, though. I imagine there is a lot to do to organize something like that for first-time campers."

He squinted one eye. "Like you?"

She laughed. "You still think you're going to make a mountain woman out of me?"

"Stranger things have happened."

"Don't hold your breath."

"I can be very persuasive." He *did* look determined.

"So get used to the idea of finding yourself signed, sealed and delivered to an upcoming outdoor adventure."

Signed, sealed…

Her breath caught and she clapped her hand to her mouth, her eyes rounding as they met his. "Oh, no!"

His eyes twinkled. "Oh, yes."

She shook her head. "No, I mean—signed, sealed and delivered. Sawyer, I forgot to mail your envelope yesterday. I stuck it in my jacket pocket and—I'm sorry. Luke and I got talking and neither of us remembered."

She pulled the folded envelope from her pocket and handed it to him. "I'm so—"

"Sawyer! Sawyer!" Landon's voice cut through the still-chilly air as he raced from around the back of the house, then called to his twin behind him. "Come on, Cubby! Sawyer's here."

Quick as a flash, their big brother opened the truck door and slung the photo album bags inside. Slammed the door. Just in time, for the laughing boys were on him in an instant, engulfing him in hugs.

Chapter Nine

That night, still irritated with Ray's stance on conversations involving the twins' dad and the lost opportunity to broach the subject of a camping trip, Sawyer stayed late at the Outpost. Going over the accounting records, he'd added the payment's expected late penalty to the computerized spreadsheet of expenses.

Again, his own fault.

He should have posted the check himself or at least mentioned to Tori that it had to be postmarked that day. But no, pride had gotten in the way and he hadn't wanted her to know how carefully he was having to time the release of payments to his creditors. He'd cut it close on this one and it had come back to bite him.

By Tuesday morning, though, he'd stopped beating himself up, recalling Tori's encouraging words of a few weeks ago. She'd said it had been her observation that people who have a passion for something always find a way. She *knew* he would, too.

Stated it as a fact.

He shook his head as he adjusted the angle of the new display case according to Tori's suggestion. She hardly knew him, though, so he shouldn't take her comments to heart as much as he had. But somehow, the reminder of her words drew him up short. That was the kind of encouraging talk Dad gave him when he'd majorly messed up right after college.

It wasn't that he'd gotten in with a *bad* crowd in his undergrad years. The guys and gals were fun. High-spirited. None of them had seen any harm in weekend jaunts to Las Vegas from Flagstaff where they attended Northern Arizona University.

But he'd taken to enjoying it a little too much, hadn't drawn the line when his college days were over. Being the owner of a growing business at such a young age had been a heady experience. When, however, he started missing payments and vendors demanded their money prior to delivery, the impeccable reputation he'd inherited from his grandfather started to lose its shine. It was having his brand-new pickup repossessed that finally opened his eyes to the fact that he could lose the Outpost, too.

Which was why, five years after he'd cut himself off from gambling, he still drove a used older-model pickup. It was a daily reminder of where he'd been and where he had no intention of ever going again. Which was what made his current situation all the more frustrating. None of this financial upheaval was his own fault. Yet how many would believe that?

The cowbell above the door jangled loudly and he looked up from cleaning the glass on the new display case, his spirits lifting as Tori stepped through the door.

"That display is perfect there, Sawyer."

"Your idea." He gave the glass a final swipe with a cloth, unable to resist a welcoming smile. "What are you doing here?"

"Therese took the boys in for their dental checkups, so I'm running errands with my unexpected free time."

"And…?"

"And I wanted to stop by and let you know I talked to Ray and Therese last night."

"About…?"

"Camping."

He wished she hadn't done that. He wadded the polishing cloth and dropped it on top of the case. Camping with the boys was his to deal with. If anyone had the rock-solid experience to win the Selbys over, it was him. Now she'd gone and stolen—probably forfeited—his only opportunity to present a credible proposal.

Folding his arms, he leaned his hip against the case. "Earlier you said the timing was wrong."

"It was. But last night at dinner Landon let it slip about wanting to go camping with you."

"I was afraid of that." He raised his hand, then with a low, spiraling whistle, arched it over and downward in a classic crash and burn motion. He couldn't blame her, though. Not if the boys jumped the gun. But if he'd been there, might he have been able to redeem the situation? "Thanks for trying, Tori."

A crease formed between her brows. "I did more than try."

"I'm sure you did. It's not your fault."

"What's not my fault?"

"That Ray and Therese put the kibosh on it."

She laughed and stepped up to him, grabbing a fistful of fabric on the front of his shirt. "Oh, ye of little faith."

He clasped his hand around her fist, startled at the softness cradled in his palm. "You're telling me they said *yes*?"

"They said they'd think about it. And talk to you."

"You're kidding me."

Eyes dancing, she moved her head slowly back and forth. "Nope."

He didn't know whether to hug her or... His gaze dropped to her smiling lips and his heart did an excruciating rollover.

She must have picked up on where his unruly mind was going, for uncertainty flickered through her eyes as she abruptly unfisted her fingers. Slipped her hand from his. Stepped back. "So the rest is up to you, mountain man."

"I don't know what to say, except thanks."

"It's not a done deal yet." She paced the floor, almost skittishly. "But after the twins left the table, I did explain how this would be a good experience and that you hadn't made any promises to the boys. I made sure they understood, too, that it was Cubby and Landon's idea, not yours. And that you wanted to talk to Ray and Therese first before any plans were made."

"Sounds as if you covered the bases."

"I mentioned, too, that you're thinking of inviting several others who have children. That you thought Ray and Therese might like to go along." She cringed slightly. "I hope that was okay."

He couldn't imagine either of them wanting to rough it, but Ray might decide it expedient to tag along and ensure the big brother didn't reminisce about the father he shared with Cubby and Landon. He'd deal with it, though. Make the best of it should it come to that.

"The more the merrier."

She gave him a quick smile. "Good."

"This is quite a turnaround from how things looked Saturday. I guess I should give them a call?"

"Strike while the iron's hot."

"Thanks for laying the groundwork on this one. I'll

check with Luke and Delaney and Grady and Sunshine first, though. Make sure they're interested before I commit them to anything."

"Good idea. But I imagine it won't take much persuasion to bring Sunshine on board. Like me, she didn't have much of an outdoorsy upbringing. As a new Hunter Ridge town council member who's attempting to bridge the tension between the artist newcomers and die-hard outdoorsmen, she'll be eager to gain a better understanding of that vital element of the community. Camping will further expand her horizons."

"And yours? You've been evasive on committing to this yourself." Why was it important to him that Tori join them? So he could show off what a rough and tough outdoorsman he was?

"I'm still considering it."

"You know if you agree to go, that will weigh in favor with Ray and Therese's decision. They're more likely to say yes to the boys going knowing you'll be along, too."

"That's not fair to put that kind of pressure on me."

"No pressure. And I promise I won't make you clean a fish or bait any hooks."

She placed her hands on her hips, looking somewhat offended. "You think I couldn't handle that?"

"Something has you riding the fence."

"Well, it's not that."

"Oh, yeah? Then what is it? Spit it out and whatever it is, I'll make it good. Ease your fears."

There was absolutely nothing Sawyer Banks could do to ease her fears. And she had no intention of sharing what they were. What woman wanted to tell a man she'd known only a month that she'd dreamed of him more than once in recent days? Woke up in the morning smiling before the dream fully faded?

All she knew was that she couldn't allow herself to be drawn into the whirlpool of attraction to Sawyer. Not when she was beginning to take control of her own life again. Getting involved with someone new, so soon after Heath, wasn't a wise move. She couldn't allow herself to become distracted from her new job and the sewing projects that would get her foot in the door at the Hunter Ridge Artists' Co-op. There was no doubt in her mind that Sawyer had the potential to be a major distraction.

She'd permitted her former fiancé to do too much of that, influencing her to gradually let go of the business she'd shared with her grandmother. After all, as he'd pointed out, quilting was a fine *hobby*, but they were on their way to becoming partners in business, partners in love, partners in life. So she'd willingly invested time, money and creative energy, relinquishing her own dreams to make *his* dreams for a successful restaurant come true.

And then, as the restaurant gained popularity, he'd said he needed "some breathing room." The next thing she knew, he was sending her on her way—making it clear, ironically, that she didn't have a life of her own. He needed, he'd explained, a woman who could stand on her own two feet.

"Tori?" Sawyer's voice jerked her to the present. He was gazing at her quizzically. "You're going to make me guess what's holding you back from a camping trip?"

"There's nothing to guess," she stated firmly. She certainly didn't want him trying. "I have no fears related to camping. You have my word on that."

"Then you'll go?"

"If Therese and Ray say yes to the boys going, I'll go."

But would she later come to regret it?

* * *

"I'm still dumbfounded." Sawyer shook his head as he wandered the floor of the Outpost, his cell phone pressed to his ear late the following Friday morning. "You must have expertly set the stage, Tori. As I'm sure you know by now, last night Ray got back to me. He voiced a few concerns he'd earlier shared with you, but I compromised because I think it's important to get the boys into outdoor activities."

Maybe Tori's prayers had had an impact as well as her words? It wasn't, however, as if Ray had dropped the somewhat distant approach he reserved for dealing with his grandsons' older brother. Sawyer wisely hadn't broached the subject of sharing family photos with his siblings. That could wait until later.

"Therese did fill me in." She sounded excited. "I'm relieved they're going along with this. When do you plan to tell the boys?"

"I want to get everything planned out first. Check the long-term weather. Next week ushers in April, but it can still get nippy enough to snow."

"The least amount of time the boys have to wait after you tell them, the better." He could hear the smile in her voice and found his own smile surfacing. "Time flies for adults, but not for children."

"My thoughts exactly." He'd called to let her know he'd gotten the official go-ahead, but was curiously reluctant to draw the conversation to a close. "Thanks again for your help."

"I was happy to. Anything else you need to cover with me?"

She must have things she needed to get back to. "Not offhand."

"While I have you here, then…do you know where Snowshoe Road is?"

"Yeah, why?"

"I'm going out there this afternoon. A woman I met at church who does quilt finishing invited me to her place to take a look at her work. I have a number of quilt tops put together and I'm looking for someone who does finish work."

Snowshoe Road. Kyle and his wife lived out there. Crazy remote area.

"You're not talking about trying to find the Guthridge place, are you?"

"You know Annie?"

"Annie and Kyle. Sure. Kyle and I worked together at Hunter's Hideaway in the summer when we were teenagers. Then roomed together in college."

"Small world," she marveled. "And yes, that's where I'm off to this afternoon."

"You'll never find it," he couldn't help but tease. "Either that or you'll never find your way home."

"I have a GPS on my phone," she defended. "And Annie gave me directions."

He chuckled. "Then you'll definitely never find it."

"I *have* to go. I've made an appointment for two o'clock." She paused, hopefully to reconsider, but he detected a stubborn lilt in her next words. "At least I've heard this area has a top-notch search-and-rescue team."

"It does. I'm on it."

"You are? Then wish me *bon voyage* for now," she stated cheerfully. He could picture the soft curve of her smile. "And I guess I'll see you and your team later."

"Wait! Don't hang up." She was serious about going despite his warnings? Well, he was serious, too. She had no business wandering around out there on her own. "That road isn't for the fainthearted—or Kia compacts."

"The Selbys' SUV is in the shop for servicing."

"You can't wait a day or two until it's out?" But even in a four-wheel drive that place wasn't easy to locate. The road often washed out in the spring with winter snowmelt, too.

"Annie had a cancellation. So there's an opening right now to get my quilts finished, and I intend to take it."

It didn't sound as if there would be any point in arguing. While he couldn't afford the time away from the Outpost to play backcountry chauffeur, no way was he letting her go out to Kyle and Annie's by herself. Especially not in that low-slung car of hers.

"You said the appointment's for two o'clock, right? I'll pick you up at one fifteen."

"But—"

"No buts." He kept his voice firm. "I can't risk losing my valuable Outpost assistant right now. One fifteen sharp."

Something in his tone must have stopped her in her tracks for, surprisingly, she didn't argue.

When he arrived at the Selbys' place he didn't have long to wait for Therese and Ray's front door to open. But instead of an expected rowdy welcome from the twins, Tori stood just inside, a fleeting emotion he couldn't put his finger on flickering through her eyes. Had she changed her mind about going? Or had his arrival interrupted something? From that look on her face, she'd definitely been thrown out of the saddle.

He frowned. "What's wrong?"

Chapter Ten

Tori stared at Sawyer for a long moment, still stunned by what Therese and Ray had shared with her moments before Sawyer rang the bell.

Multiple sclerosis.

They'd known for years, keeping it from friends and family. But they'd talked it over and decided Tori needed to know. Too often over the past month she'd witnessed Therese's sudden weakness, tremors, dizziness, chronic fatigue and mood swings. With Tori living under their roof, they said, it was becoming too difficult to hide. It wasn't fair to her to leave her in the dark, and attempting to conceal it was becoming too stressful for them.

"What makes you think something's wrong?"

"You look—"

She fisted a hand on her hip. "Now don't go telling a woman she isn't looking well, Sawyer. Surely you know better than that."

"Are you ready to go, then?"

"Just let me grab my stuff."

She left him standing on the porch, pausing in the kitchen doorway long enough to remind Therese and

Ray she'd be back in time to pick up the boys from pre-school afterward.

Ray nodded. "We'll visit again when you return. I'm sure you have questions."

"But please remember—" Therese managed a wan smile, as if the effort of having shared her long-held secret had further tired her "—not to share this with anyone. We're not ready to go public with the details of my health."

"I understand." But the moment the truth had come out—not solely arthritis but MS—Tori's thoughts had flown to her promise to Sawyer. A promise to share with him anything she thought could negatively impact the welfare of the twins.

Was this one of those things?

In her apartment, she slipped into her jacket and snatched three garbage-size plastic bags filled with her quilting. When she met Sawyer at his truck, he helped her in, then shut the door and climbed into the driver's side.

"All set?" He studied her for a moment as if still not convinced there wasn't something wrong. But he didn't say anything more, for which she was grateful.

"All set. Thanks for doing this." She knew the sacrifice he was making to be away from the Outpost.

He started the truck. "Believe me, a GPS wouldn't have a clue when it comes to finding Kyle and Annie's place. It's beyond remote. A four-wheel drive comes in handy this time of year, too." He glanced down at the bags piled between them. "So those are your quilts?"

"The base fabric and trim fabric are in this one." She patted one bag, then opened the other two so he could see the contents. "These are the tops."

"Nice colors. Woodsy."

"That was intentional." She looked back at the house

as they pulled away, silent prayers for Ray and Therese foremost in her thoughts, then focused on the conversation at hand. "It seemed 'woodsy' might be a good sales angle here in Hunter Ridge. Play up the outdoors."

"So Annie takes the top you pieced together and sews it to the solid bottom?"

"With filler between for warmth and loft. She does the actual quilting. I don't have the space or equipment to do that for something this large. These are queen-size coverlets—with matching pillow shams. I'm fortunate that there's someone locally who does finish work."

"I had no idea Kyle's wife had a business like that."

"There's a quilters guild in Canyon Springs that meets once a month. She's invited me to join and come speak to the group this summer on determining value and pricing."

"Important things to know." He nodded thoughtfully, keeping his eyes on the road. "You don't want to price yourself out of business or give your hours of creative labor away for a pittance."

"Exactly. And she's invited me to join her on a northern Arizona quilt shop tour this summer, too. I guess it's an annual regional event."

"Kyle and Annie are good folks. I'm sure you'll enjoy her company." He paused, then gave her a sideways glance as they started down a gravel side road. "So what are the boys up to this afternoon? I'd expected to fend them off when I rang the doorbell."

"The boys are at an additional day of preschool. They didn't want to miss out on today's games and art projects. Story time."

"With those kinds of offerings, I'll have to ramp up my camping plans. The boys may find hiking around in the woods and waiting for a fish to bite dull in comparison."

She playfully poked his arm. "Doubtful."

He grinned. "Well, bring an age-appropriate book just in case, will you? Something about wildlife maybe."

"That will be unnecessary, I can assure you."

"I'm still recovering from the fact that after they had a few days to think about it, Ray didn't put up much of an argument. Therese none at all."

But Ray *had* told her Sawyer had agreed to honor his concerns—up to a point. He wouldn't initiate a conversation, but if the boys asked him questions about their mom and dad, he would respond. Therese was fine with that. Ray less so, but he gave the go-ahead nevertheless—and hadn't said a word about coming along himself.

Had Ray given thought to what she'd talked to him about earlier? That in order to emotionally heal, the boys needed the freedom to speak about what was on their minds and how they felt. Or perhaps his concerns about Therese's health were occupying most of his time and attention.

Farther on, she winced as the truck bumped through yet another road-wide pothole, and gratitude rose that she wasn't out here on her own. If Sawyer stopped right now and asked her to drive them home, she was so turned around that she couldn't have. "I see why you had your doubts as to my finding this place. This so-called road would have ripped the bottom right out of my Kia."

He'd also had to put his truck into four-wheel drive to pull through a low-lying quagmire of mud more than once.

"I've been out here plenty of times and it's worse in the winter and spring. Or after a monsoon rain. But it's always easy enough to get turned around. Especially at night."

She shuddered at the thought of being out here in the dark.

They continued to bump along, the time adding up,

with their speed not much above fifteen or twenty miles an hour over rubboard roads. Every time she'd start to relax, they'd jolt through a small crater or over another rough patch, forcing her to brace herself—or she'd be brought up short by the memory of Therese's health revelation. *Was* that something Sawyer needed to know? But Ray and Therese made a point of asking her not to share the news with anyone.

Please, God, give me wisdom.

"Here we are," Sawyer said at long last, nodding to a clearing up ahead where a two-story cabin with solar panels on the roof and a wisp of smoke curling from a stone chimney looked quite homey. A barn, corral with a few horses, and other outbuildings were scattered across the property. Off to one side she spied huge poly tanks—people living this far out had to haul in water—and in a sunny spot were raised garden beds awaiting spring planting. Annie seemed an "earth mother" type, and this place didn't disappoint.

While Sawyer didn't strike her as the potential mate of an Annie type, he was probably on the lookout for a woman who could hold her own on one of those reality TV survival programs. One who could hike all day without breaking a sweat, build a shelter from scratch with the aid of a pocketknife, start a fire without matches and still manage to catch and clean a bucket of fish and fry them up for supper.

Not, of course, that what he was looking for was any of her business.

"I'm glad to see you didn't attempt to come out on your own, Tori." Tucking a strand of hair back into her ponytail, Annie Guthridge motioned them into the house, a welcoming smile lighting her rosy-cheeked, round face.

Sawyer's buddy Kyle had hit the jackpot when he found his easygoing life partner. Not that she let him get away with much, but they were an ideal match, each the president of the other's fan club.

"The last snowfall melting," she continued, "gummed up the roads. You'll have to get that truck of yours to the car wash when you get back, Sawyer."

"Plan on it." But washing the pickup was the last thing on his mind with the aroma of freshly baked bread and something beefy in a crockpot scenting the air. No wonder Kyle had put on a few extra pounds in recent years.

She pointed to a wide doorway. "Take your stuff right in there, Tori, and let's have a look at it."

Tori preceded them, oohing and aahing at a magnificent quilt stretched across a frame in the adjoining room. But Annie held back to grab Sawyer's arm and whisper in his ear. "Kyle said you had a new lady friend."

A bolt of alarm jolted through him, his words barely audible. "She's not—"

"Annie! This is gorgeous!" Tori's voice held the usual upbeat lilt he'd become accustomed to, reminding him that, oddly, it had seldom surfaced on their drive to the Guthridge place. The "not right" feeling that had struck him when she'd first opened the Selbys' door still lingered.

His friend's wife joined Tori and together they moved around the room, Annie explaining her background and processes and showing off several types of sewing machines. From what he could make of it, a Bernina was a good thing.

Rightly guessing that this might take a while, he settled into a recliner in the corner—Kyle's spot if he wanted to spend time with his wife when she was neck-deep in a project? Tori then spread out her quilt tops and discussion continued. He took it from Annie's comments that she was impressed with Tori's work, so it wasn't only his amateur eye that discerned they were compelling designs.

Theme. Mood. Presentation. Fiber content. Technique. He didn't understand much of it, but found it interesting nevertheless. There was more to this quilting business than he'd supposed. Tori spoke knowledgeably, too. Knew this quilting gig as thoroughly as he did his outdoors one.

But he also had another motive for listening in—to make certain Annie didn't further allude to a presumed relationship with Tori. Under other circumstances, Annie's obvious excitement at the prospect might not have put him so much on edge as it had. Tori was smart. Fun. Talented. She loved his little brothers—and tolerated him. He enjoyed her company more than he should. But he was in no way financially anchored well enough to go looking for a lady. His taking this break from work today with a notion of keeping her safe was evidence, if only in a small way, of how time-consuming a relationship would be. Time he needed to spend bringing the Outpost ledgers back into the black.

An hour later they headed back out the door...Annie giving him an audacious wink when Tori wasn't looking.

He shook his head, but couldn't restrain a smile. She and Kyle had been on his case for several years now to start dating again, insisting it was time to put the memories of the past behind him. He no longer gambled. He no longer hung out with Vegas groupies who'd trailed him and his buddies around in hopes of landing themselves a high-stakes winner. Not that any of the guys ever came close to attaining anything like that. But the girls still hoped.

But with that part of his life behind him, he'd chosen to focus on the outdoors, on the Outpost, on renovating his cabin—and spending time with Dad and Vanessa and the boys.

That is, up until the fire.

Nearing town, he realized Tori hadn't been talking as excitedly as he would have expected about her encounter with Kyle's wife or Annie having invited her to coteach a beginner's quilting class at the church that summer. In fact, their conversation consisted of not much more than taking turns commenting on the passing scenery or the deplorable condition of the winding roads.

It was as if, as he earlier suspected, she still had something on her mind. But he hadn't been much of a conversationalist either. The *reality* of what the well-meaning Annie and Kyle obviously hoped to be a blossoming new relationship weighed heavily. What his two friends didn't get was that he didn't have anything to offer a woman at this point in his life, let alone anything to offer someone like the sparkling gem sitting next to him in quiet contemplation.

Looking for a distraction from his thoughts, he turned on the radio to pull in the familiar country rhythm of an old Alan Jackson tune.

Tori perked up. "You like Alan Jackson?"

"Forever."

"Me, too." Humming along, she turned up the volume as if also welcoming a diversion from wherever her thoughts had taken her.

"I don't suppose…" he started, then shook his head. He still sensed something was bothering her and would like to cheer her up. But he needed to keep his head in Outpost business and not get ahead of himself. Maybe, if she was still around come next fall…maybe when he got the bills paid off…

She tilted her head. "What?"

"Nothing. Thinking out loud."

For a moment he thought she was going to say something, but to his disappointment she settled into her seat to once again stare out the window.

While he still regularly offered up thanks, he hadn't asked God for much, if anything, in the past year. Didn't see much point in it. But as his gaze again drifted to Tori, lingered on her delicate profile, the soft blond hair, the gentle, pensive expression in her eyes…he couldn't help but wonder if maybe he needed to rethink that decision…

Chapter Eleven

"Curtis, there is no need for you to come here. That's exactly why your father and I didn't say anything earlier." From across the kitchen a week and a half after the trip to Annie's, Therese gave Tori an exasperated look as her son continued talking to her on the landline. Then she shook her head. "No, let's not revisit that. You know how we feel about relocating to LA. You kids can get that out of your heads."

With breakfast over and Ray and the twins out the door, Tori finished cleaning up, trying not to eavesdrop. But she nevertheless picked up on the tension in Therese's voice.

On Sunday Therese and Ray had called each of their offspring individually to share Therese's diagnosis with them, and it sounded from this call as if their children had gotten together and her oldest son was now voicing their combined concerns.

Tori knew they'd wanted their parents to relocate to where the three lived within an hour's drive of each other. Now that they knew of their mother's developing health issues, that effort was being renewed. Would Therese and Ray consider it? They'd have to take the boys with them, of course, which would devastate Sawyer. And *she'd* be out of a job.

Tori hadn't been back at her sewing too long before a laughing Therese knocked at the open door, making a face and pretending to pull her hair out. "I told Ray that telling the kids would open a can of worms. But I think I have Curtis convinced that he doesn't need to come over here to 'talk some sense into us,' as he put it."

"They care for you. Want what's best for you."

"But they aren't telling us anything we don't know. This house was way too big for us after our children grew up and moved out. But even though it's full of happy memories—and a few sad ones—" she was obviously thinking of her daughter, the twins' mother "—it had been our intent to eventually sell, get a trailer or cabin here for summer months and then winter in Phoenix at one of those senior retirement resorts. Ray and I both love to golf and swim."

"Some of those places come with awesome perks."

"They do. And quite honestly, we weren't around that much when Cubby and Landon were tiny. We traveled a lot. Visited our kids and grandkids. But when the boys came to live with us, of course, we tabled those plans and activities." She moved closer to see what Tori was working on and nodded approvingly. "We raised four kids in a small town and think Hunter Ridge is still ideal. But with two growing boys who will be teenagers in the blink of an eye, we can't downsize a great deal now either."

Teenagers in the blink of an eye. Tori almost shuddered at the thought. "Your kids know, don't they, that you'd be bringing the boys if you moved to California?"

"That's part of the push to move closer to them. They think the twins are too much for us. Baloney. We're doing fine."

But Tori could understand the Selby children's concerns. The boys took time and energy. Money, too. It was clear from what she'd picked up on from Ray and Therese and others as well, that their social life, church and community involvement, and leisure activities had been greatly curtailed in the past year. Friends complained of seldom seeing them.

"That's where you've been such a blessing, Tori, and I reminded Curtis of that." Therese smiled at her. "You've taken charge of many things that previously might have been stretching us to our limits. I feel good about where we are, even with this MS hanging over my head. Ray and I feel confident in standing our ground to remain in Hunter Ridge. While we didn't grow up here, this has been the home of our hearts."

Despite her employer's optimistic spirit, an undercurrent of uneasiness surfaced. "You need to be sure, Therese, to let me know if there's more I can do to help you. Not just with the kids, but with everyday things you might find tiring."

"We hired you to watch after the twins, not be a health-care aide."

"I know, but friends help friends."

Therese's gaze softened. "And we are becoming friends, aren't we?"

"We are."

"I'll keep your offer in mind, but despite what our worrywart kids think, things are working out." Therese moved to the table where Tori's finished items were beginning to stack up and lifted one of the baby quilts. "You've been turning out the work. I used to do a little quilting myself. You know, from one of those kits that come with the fabric precut. I'm amazed you choose the color combinations and fabric on your own. No pattern to follow."

Tori laughed. "I follow a pattern that's in my head."

"You're a gifted artist. It's a shame you can't do this full-time."

"I will. Someday. But it will take time to get there."

Therese looked at her fondly. "I don't doubt you will. You're young. Determined. Like Sawyer in that respect, who thinks the sky is the limit."

Therese drifted toward the door, then paused. "I know I mentioned this the other day, but I do appreciate you not saying anything to anyone—including Sawyer—about my health. I don't need him doubting that I'm capable of caring for his siblings."

Tori took a steadying breath. It hadn't been easy not saying anything to Sawyer about Therese's occasional brain fog. A faucet left running or an opened medication bottle on the countertop. But health issues were personal and if she hadn't been working here she'd never have been made aware of those things. Which was why she'd determined to be as diligent as possible in keeping the boys safe and bringing potentially harmful situations to the attention of the Selbys, as she'd already been faithfully doing.

"He'd be concerned, Therese—for you."

Therese's gentle smile held a tinge of disbelief. "He'd be concerned I'm sure—concerned that my health might go belly-up entirely and he'd get stuck with the kids himself. He's next in line in the will for taking on the boys, you know. But I'm not sure much troubles that young man as long as it doesn't impact him."

"Why do you say that?" She hadn't known the twins' parents had included Sawyer in their contingency plans.

The older woman studied her. "You like him, don't you?"

Tori's face warmed. "He's nice. A good boss. He loves his little brothers."

"Just be careful."

"I think you're wrong about him. But you needn't worry about me. I came out of a deeply disappointing relationship not that many months ago and I'm in no hurry to get myself into another one."

At least that's what she kept telling herself.

"I'm glad to hear you're taking your time. God has someone special in mind for you." Therese placed her hand to her heart. "I feel it right here."

When she left, Tori returned to her sewing, but found it hard to concentrate. She didn't like keeping things from Sawyer that might impact him and the boys. The MS diagnosis. The pressure to move to California. But Therese and Ray had no intention of leaving Hunter Ridge, despite their children's urging, so for the time being at least, that was a nonissue. Should things change, if Therese and Ray reconsidered a move to California, then she'd speak up.

And yet…what good would that do?

The Selbys had legal custody of the boys and it was doubtful they'd consider relinquishing that to a bachelor older brother who'd personally assured Tori he had no interest in or intention of trying to take the boys from their grandparents. Even Sunshine had laughed when Tori shared concerns that he might be setting her up to "get the goods" on the boys' grandparents so he could use her testimony in court to gain custody.

Tori adjusted the fabric under the sewing machine's foot. She'd seen no signs that Sawyer was working toward taking the boys from their grandparents. In fact, it was at *her* urging that he was becoming more involved in their lives.

The good news, too, was that with the Selbys determined to raise their grandsons in Hunter Ridge, she had housing and a job for a while. Maybe clear through their grade school years. She could continue to be closely involved in the lives of Cubby and Landon.

And that of their big brother?

Giving attention again to her sewing, she shook away that intruding thought, not sure where it had come from. Yes, as Therese had observed, she did like him. But *liking*...well, she liked a lot of people, right?

She was here in Hunter Ridge for the twins and the twins alone.

"Keep backing up, Cubby!" Sawyer's voice carried across the tree-lined open space at the city park nestled in the heart of Hunter Ridge's business district. He sidestepped Landon, who was trying to keep him from throwing the football.

It was hard to stay focused, though, with a laughing Tori playfully running back and forth in front of Cubby, waving her hands as if determined to gain an interception. With the sun high overhead, raising the April early-afternoon temperature to at least fifty degrees, she'd earlier tossed her jacket on top of a nearby picnic table. In trim jeans and a fitted ocean-blue sweater, sunlight illuminating her blond hair, she was distracting, that was for sure.

With Landon moving in on him again, Sawyer sent the football gently arcing toward Cubby, confident he'd hit his target if his little brother would stretch out his arms. But the boy froze.

"Catch it, Cub!"

Abruptly, the boy thrust out his arms and, as the ball landed in them, he hugged the pigskin to his chest as Sawyer had shown him in practice.

Cubby's grin widened. "I caught it! I caught it!"

Spotting Tori's amused look, Sawyer laughed. "You did, buddy, but don't stand there. Run!"

The boy's eyes widened, then still hugging the ball he turned and took off toward their opponents' goal.

"No, Cub, the other way!"

Making a wide arc Cubby swung around and headed in the right direction. But not far from the goal line Landon snagged the red bandanna from his back pocket. Cubby kept moving, though, right over the sticks marking an end zone, and did his own version of a victory dance.

"That doesn't count," Landon complained loudly, looking in disgust to Sawyer. "I had the bandanna."

"You're right. It doesn't count, but he's put us in a great position, so heads up, defensive line."

Cubby trotted up to him for a high five, then handed over the ball. Man, did he love these brothers. It was encouraging, too, to see Cubby enjoying himself. Gaining confidence. Acting more like he had before his parents died—back when the world seemed a happier place to be.

An invisible weight settled into Sawyer's heart just as a cloud passed over the sun, throwing the park below into shadow. The wind picked up, piercing through his cotton T-shirt. How his dad would have loved being out here on a day like this, playing flag football with his sons, Vanessa cheering from the sidelines.

But that would never happen, would it?

He squared his shoulders and shook off the haunting reminder as he instructed Cubby on their next play. The little guy performed like a pro and over the goal line he went, this time officially scoring.

"Tie!" Tori hollered as she gave Landon a hug, then opened her arms to Cubby, who, having tossed the ball to Landon, came running to get one, too.

Maybe he should queue up, as well? Get a victory hug from the cute blonde? Mighty tempting.

With a pang of regret, Sawyer glanced at his watch. Good place to call it a day. "Sorry, guys, but it's time for me to get back to the Outpost."

"Awww." Landon trudged toward him, tossing the football from one hand to the other. "We don't get a chance to break the tie?"

"Not today."

"Bummer." But Cubby's eyes were still bright from his touchdown.

"Maybe tomorrow if the weather's good." For the past week, he'd started eating his lunch later, timing it around Tori and the boys' postlunch park outing. She didn't seem to mind the intrusion and he did love time with his brothers. Yeah, being around them still hurt. Worse on some days. But it was great to no longer hold himself back, gnawed by guilt.

He had Tori to thank for this renewed opportunity to bond with his brothers. He enjoyed spending time with her outside the store, too. Often Les or Diego were around when she was there, so they didn't have that much time to talk in private. At least on days like this when the boys were on the park swings or a slide, he'd snatch a few minutes to chat with her. Find out how her day was going. How the boys were doing.

He'd hoped she'd be more confiding in him about the day-to-day goings-on at the house, but she seemed determined to stick to her original resolution that she'd only tell him of anything she thought might be of a serious enough nature to impact the boys negatively. So far, nothing.

Which meant, as he'd been beginning to suspect, his concerns for the boys' welfare, his perceptions of their unhappiness in the big old house, were mostly in his imagination—a lingering aftermath of the guilt that had weighed on him since the moment he'd heard the cause of the fire.

Tori abruptly made her presence known as she bumped his arm with hers. "Why so glum? Staring off into space wondering what happened to your victory? A tie isn't the end of the world, but you thought you could beat us, didn't you?"

The boys were now chasing each other, making a game of trying to see who could maintain possession of the ball. He gazed down at her and his heartbeat accelerated. She was so pretty, looking up at him with starry-lashed eyes, her face flushed from the exertion of the game. But it wasn't just how she looked that drew him. He'd known plenty of attractive women. She was *special*, for want of a better word. Kind. Gentle. Fun.

"With Cubby on your side," she prodded, "you thought you'd whup us. That kid is a hidden gold mine."

"He seems to be coming out of hiding more and more, doesn't he? Not all the time. But more often."

"He is. Good to see."

She took a few steps to the picnic table, where she retrieved her jacket. He helped her on with it, sensing that there was something else she wanted to say. He didn't have long to wait.

"I've noticed you've made an effort to join the boys on our park outings several times this week."

"My schedule lent itself to it. It won't always."

"Cubby and Landon love it. They've talked about it every night at mealtime."

He shifted uncomfortably. It wasn't like he thought he could keep the time spent with them a secret from their grandparents. That wasn't his intention, but somehow knowing that the couple was being regaled with stories about him made him uneasy. "How does that go over with Ray and Therese? Probably not real thrilled, right?"

"Why do you say that?"

Why *did* he say that? Maybe because of the way they both looked at him. As if not quite trusting him. He'd long feared that Dad's wife might have shared with them the gambling trouble Sawyer had found himself in, the questionable lifestyle, or at least that they'd heard rumors around town about it. But thankfully it appeared they didn't know the truth of the part he'd played in their daughter's death.

"I've never been convinced they like me much, that maybe they think I'm a bad influence. I mean, here they have these cute grandkids who have this big bad brother a quarter of a century older. Like I said before, for some reason I make them uncomfortable."

"Have you tried to talk to them about it? Clear the air? Maybe there's nothing to it."

Why did he get the feeling *Tori* thought there might be something to it?

"I hope you don't mind my asking, Sawyer, but—" *okay, here it comes* "—why is it you're overly concerned about the boys living with their grandparents? And pardon me for feeling paranoid, but it seems that you appearing here in the park each day recently is an indication that you don't trust me to keep my part of our bargain."

Caught off guard, Sawyer's breath caught as he stared

into her questioning eyes. He couldn't exactly confess, could he, that in addition to enjoying time with his little brothers…he wanted to spend more time with her, too?

Chapter Twelve

There. She'd said it. Maybe now he'd explain why she kept picking up on half-said things from both the Selbys and Sawyer himself. Confirm that her instincts were spot-on.

He shifted slightly, as if uncomfortable with her questions. "You have that all wrong, Tori. I trust you. Okay, maybe at first I was uncertain when you turned the tables on me. But you've proven yourself. More than proven yourself. I'm counting on you."

Did her uneasiness, then, stem solely from her own guilty feelings? From not running to him with everything that occurred in the Selby household that pricked her conscience? But she'd addressed the issues—the stove-top burner left on, the unsecured meds—so what would be the point in alarming him?

"Okay. But why do I sense this…" How to explain it? "This wall between you and the Selbys? They don't talk about it. You don't talk about it. But I'd have to be blind not to see it."

His gaze drifted to the boys, now joined by a few other children at the swings.

"I can't tell you what you're picking up on from the

Selbys. But I can admit that while I didn't recognize it until now—" he looked as if he didn't relish having to say what he intended to tell her "—maybe it's more about me than them."

She tilted her head, not understanding.

"You know my dad was a widower, who later married the Selbys' daughter. But what you probably don't know is that his first wife—my mother—died thirteen years before he remarried."

Tori mentally ran the calculations. "When you were a young boy."

"Just turning eleven."

"I had no idea that, like your brothers, you lost your mother at such a young age. I'm so sorry."

"Yeah, well, I was older. As in the case with my dad, I have more memories. More to hold on to than those two little fellas do." He watched them playing, swinging higher and higher, their laughter filling the air. "So I know what it's like to be motherless. I know how empty I felt for the longest time. Abandoned, even."

She lightly touched his arm. "So you think you're transposing your feelings on to your brothers' situation? Subconsciously attempting to—"

"To hold their grandparents accountable for the less-than-happy days I'd sometimes observed when seeing the boys around town, I can admit now that maybe my own history is coloring my impressions."

"Maybe the Selbys sense that." That could account for them distancing themselves from him. Kind of like when you detect that someone expects the worst of you and you find yourself floundering in the very ways they unfairly presumed you would. Had they pulled back, sensing what they perceived as his disapproval? Therese mentioned not long ago, hadn't she, that she didn't need him doubting she was capable of caring for her grandsons?

Looking at it from both perspectives, it made sense. Hurting people hurt others without intending to. But maybe she could somehow bridge the gap between the three adults who shared a common bond with the orphaned brothers.

To her surprise, Sawyer lifted her chin with a gentle finger, his gaze intent. "What's going on in that head of yours? You look like you're hatching a plan or something."

"No plans. But I'm praying."

He withdrew his hand. "Have at it if it will make you feel better."

"You don't believe in the power of prayer? In God?"

"Oh, I believe in God. You can't spend as much time in the outdoors as I do and not believe there's a master plan. A Creator. It's way too complex. There's too much thought put into it to be an accident."

"But you don't pray?"

"I pray. Mostly to give thanks for what God's given me. But…"

"But what?"

"I've called out to God when it really counted. When my mother was suffering from a series of strokes that debilitated her more and more. When I saw how lost my dad was when she died." He pressed his lips together and drew a breath. "And I prayed until I thought my heart would explode while I stood out in that cold autumn night as my dad and his wife were air-vacced to Show Low, overcome by smoke inhalation. That's when I learned that while I believe in God, while I gave my life to Him not too long before my mother died…for whatever reason, God doesn't listen to me much."

"Oh, Sawyer. He does. He *does*."

"Then why are the boys' mom and dad dead?" Sawyer looked away, swallowing hard as his eyes narrowed in the direction of the twins. "I want to be there for my brothers—whatever age they are—when that same question hits them."

Her insides went cold. "And what will you tell them?"

He continued to watch the twins play. Silent. Then he turned his head slowly to look down at her, his expression bleak. "I don't have a clue."

"Well, mister," Sawyer grumbled as he climbed into his truck outside the Echo Ridge Outpost later that evening, "you sure showed Tori what you were made of this afternoon."

Man, he'd probably come across to her like some petulant child because he didn't get his way. Or at the least an ungrateful disbeliever. But that wasn't the way it was with him at all. It was just that, well, life's lessons taught him not to put too much expectation into asking for things if you didn't want to be disappointed.

How must that have sounded to Tori? And when he told her he didn't have a clue what he'd tell the boys when they asked where God had been when their parents died?

She'd said, *I'm sorry, Sawyer.*

And walked away.

It had been all he could do not to storm after her. To apologize for being such a jerk. Yet he'd returned to work, his heart aching at having disappointed her.

With a growl, he switched on the pickup's headlights, checked the nonexistent traffic and backed into the road. His stomach gnawed at his backbone. Breakfast had been a bowl of cereal. Dry. He'd forgotten to buy milk this week. Then he'd skipped lunch to spend time at the park, afterward grabbing a bag of pretzels and a soda out of his office stash.

Fast food from a drive-through didn't appeal, though. Maybe something from the Log Cabin Café. Or Rusty's Grill. If he'd have been using his noggin, he could have called ahead and they'd have had it waiting for him.

As he drove farther down the main road through town, his driver's-side window open a slit, the faint smell of burning oak wafted in on the cold night air. Barbecue. Rusty's it would be. Maybe a sandwich platter with mashed potatoes and a veggie on the side.

Inside the restaurant's rustic beamed-ceiling space, he placed a take-out order with the hostess, then seated himself in one of the wooden ladder-back chairs arranged in the waiting area. The restaurant was homey, with flickering lanterns anchored to beadboard-paneled walls and the scent of barbecued chicken, pork and beef almost enough to make his mouth water.

As Sawyer attempted to ignore the incessant screaming of a red-faced kid he guessed to be about a year old, the boy's dad smiled apologetically, bouncing the youngster on his knee, trying to distract him, but with little success.

Boy, did that racket take him back a few years to when the twins were that age. Lungs that wouldn't quit. Thankfully, Dad survived that phase and got to enjoy them for a few more years before—

"Well, look who's here—Sawyer Banks," a female voice called as a handful of young women exited the dining section of the restaurant. "What are you doing out here by your lonesome?"

Delaney Marks—or rather Delaney Hunter now— her wavy blond hair tumbling over her shoulders, came to stand in front of him, any sign of a baby bump hidden under her coat. She was due this coming summer, or so he'd heard. And behind her followed a chatting Jodi Thorpe, Sunshine Carston Hunter, Rio Hunter—and Tori Janner.

He rose to his feet. "Good evening, ladies."

Delaney folded her arms. "You didn't answer my question. You're not here by yourself, are you?"

"Just picking up a take-out order. I assume this band of merry maidens has been enjoying a ladies' night out?"

"We try to get together every month or two." Rio, Luke and Grady's youngest sister, gave him an easy smile. She'd frequented his store for years—and not for his limited supply of feminine accessories like Western-style jewelry and hand-tooled leather handbags. No, at twenty-one, she was already a crack shot and an accomplished horsewoman and hunter. But while those qualifications might be high on his list of what he always thought he'd be looking for in a mate, she'd never given him the time of day. Cute as a button, though.

With parting words, the women filed out the front door, Tori offering a hesitant smile as she passed by. But before she made it to the exit, he impulsively stepped forward to take her arm lightly and draw her to a halt. "Do you have a minute, or are you heading out for a night on the town?"

"Dinner was the extent of our plans."

"I won't keep you long." He glanced around. The baby was only whimpering now, so every eye in the room had turned to him and Tori. He didn't relish an audience. "Maybe we could step outside?"

She nodded and together they stood in the open air as her friends climbed into their vehicles. As the last one drove away, she turned to him. "So what did you need to see me about?"

"About this afternoon." He stepped aside as several couples approached the door. "Do you mind if we take a short walk? Get out of the traffic?"

She nodded and he lightly touched her elbow as they headed past a few storefronts, then turned on a side street that led in the direction of the church. He wouldn't keep her long. But somehow he had to end the day on a better note than where they'd left off.

"How's your day been?" That seemed a benign enough question to get the ball rolling.

"Good. After we went to the park, I took the boys to the library and let them select books for bedtime reading. Both picked football stories."

"I guess they had fun with the old pigskin, then?"

"They always have fun with you." She halted, her gaze in the dim light pinning him. "But you didn't ask me to take this walk to talk about football."

"No." He scuffed a booted toe on the sidewalk. "I have a confession to make. I wasn't exactly truthful with you this afternoon when I said I didn't know why Therese and Ray may not consider me a good influence for the boys."

She didn't look surprised.

"I can't say for sure, and I may be wrong. But I'm guessing it might be that they're aware of…a gambling problem."

He heard the soft catch in her breath, saw her eyes widen and immediately regretted broaching the topic.

With a kick to her gut, Tori's thoughts flew to snatches of childhood memories. Her parents' fights about money, her grandmother's candid explanations regarding their financial struggles, and the subsequent breakup of the family.

Sawyer had a gambling problem. Like her seldom-heard-from parents, who'd had no more commitment to raising a child than they had to preserving their marriage. That explained a lot, though. His overdue bills—she'd seen more than one—and Therese's and Ray's cautiousness. She couldn't brush off the legitimate concerns of the boys' grandparents.

"It's not a problem now." Studying her as though gauging her reaction, his words intruded into her thoughts. "It was at one time. During college and for a while after that. But no more."

But chronic gambling could be an addiction, couldn't it? Just like alcohol? An obsession that could raise its ugly head at any time. Or at least that had been the case for her mom and dad, who, Grandma said, were always giving it up only to turn around for one more go, thinking the next time was all it would take to resolve their financial troubles.

"In the past? What about the Vegas circulars in your junk mail basket?"

He looked slightly taken aback that she'd seen those on his kitchen counter, but she hadn't intended to snoop.

"Have you ever tried to call off the junk once they have you on a mailing list? But those are reminders of where I've been and where I don't want to be again. Nothing more."

"They're not a temptation?"

"A reminder. I got into it for the fun with my friends. The competition. The risk. Then I went overboard for a while, got caught up in the lifestyle, but after a few setbacks, a wake-up call, I recognized the direction I was heading and halted it. I wasn't a gambling addict, Tori. But it could have gone that way."

"My parents *were* gambling addicts," she said without emotion. "It destroyed their marriage. Our family."

He stared at her a long moment, processing her words.

"I'm sorry you suffered from their mistakes. Please believe me when I say I was nothing like that. I'm not like that now."

It appeared, though, that Therese and Ray still had their doubts.

But something else Sawyer had said that afternoon weighed more heavily on her thoughts than this dismaying confession. "You know, Sawyer, you're not the only one in the world who hasn't had prayers answered the way they wanted."

"I'm well aware of that."

"My parents' divorce was a traumatic event in my life," she plunged on. "And believe me, even at such a young age, I *prayed*."

"I—"

"Grandma raised me," she continued, driven to make her point. "I had a wonderful childhood and happy years with her, for the most part. And then she got sick and died. I prayed then, too. I didn't want her to die."

"Tori—"

"Late last summer things started getting bumpy with my fiancé, the man who swore up and down he'd love me forever. He said he needed some space, so I came to Hunter Ridge to help Sunshine with Tessa and give him that requested breathing room. I *prayed*. Later that fall, he dumped me. And you know what?" She poked her index finger firmly into Sawyer's solid chest. Once. Twice. "I may not have gotten everything I've dreamed of and prayed for, but when I made a commitment to God to trust Him when I was thirteen years old, I meant it."

"I'm sure—"

"I'm not telling you this to make light of your losses, Sawyer." She pushed her finger more firmly into his chest. "But I think your problem is that you're afraid to pray, to ask God to be more involved in your life because you know that might mean having to give up your self-delusion."

"My *what*?"

"The delusion that you're the one who's in control. That you call the shots. Run your universe."

From the look on his face, she could almost hear his defense mounting. *What was the point of involving God when for the most part he could handle things himself?*

Then to her surprise, he gently took her hand in his, easing the pressure on his chest. "You've given this a good deal of thought."

"I have."

"Anything else you'd like to say?"

"Plenty, probably."

"I want you to know, Tori, that when I said I wanted to be there for the boys when the same realization slams into them that slammed into me about the whys of their parents' deaths, and said I didn't know what I'd say to them, I didn't mean that in a negative way."

"Right."

"No, really. I've thought about what Dad would have wanted our relationship to be if he were here to give me guidance." He gently squeezed her hand. "I'm not their father and they'll look mostly to Ray as they grow up. But I'm serious that right at this moment I don't know what I'd tell them. How I'd explain it. Because this is an area God is working with me on and I don't have all the answers yet."

She sighed and pulled her hand away. "Sawyer, we'll never have *all* the answers."

"I'm coming to recognize that. But I guess what I'm saying is... I need you to be patient with me right now. Please don't judge. There's lots of baggage to work through."

Chapter Thirteen

If she hoped for a more reassuring response, Sawyer couldn't offer that to her. But he wanted her to know that while he wasn't there yet on trusting God, deep down he *wanted* to be. He'd long envied others their faith.

She momentarily stared down at the ground, then back up at him. "I'm sorry, Sawyer, if I've come across as judgmental. I don't mean to be."

"I know that." Why was it important that she understand, though? That she not write him off. That she not dismiss him from—what? Her mental list of potential replacements for her fiancé? Which was crazy. She was nothing like what he thought he'd be looking for in a life partner. He imagined he didn't fit the bill for her either. So why couldn't he get over that need to please her? To want her to admire him. Trust him.

"Sawyer…sometimes I sense that you're not happy with the world around you. Not happy with yourself. That concerns me. I know you don't want that rubbing off on the boys."

No, he didn't.

He'd never thought of himself as an unhappy person. Life had been good for the most part—up until the fire.

Had she picked up on the down days that he sometimes experienced because of that reality? Had the boys?

"I want you to be happy." Her words came softly, and he leaned in ever so slightly, not wanting to miss a single precious syllable.

To his surprise, with her gaze searching his, she cupped the side of his face in her hand. Warm. Soft. The sweet citrusy scent of perfume on her wrist filled his senses, heightened his awareness of her to the exclusion of all else. Shut out the chill in the air. The stars overhead. The ache in his heart.

He wanted to be happy, too. And right this minute, he felt happier than he had in a good long while. What was it about Tori that made him want to be a better man—and gave him hope that he could be?

Closing his eyes, he reached up to take her hand in his. Pressed a tender kiss to it.

He heard her soft gasp, but she didn't pull away. And when he opened his eyes once again, she was still there. Eyes wide with surprise. Lips slightly parted. She wasn't a figment of his imagination.

For a long moment, they gazed silently at each other. Could she hear his heart hammering in his chest? Did she sense how he longed to pull her into his arms? How desperately he wanted to kiss her?

He had no right to be thinking those things. They'd known each other but a short while. She'd given no indication of interest in pursuing anything but friendship. Did she sense a growing attraction between them—or was it wishful thinking on his part? Would exploring the possibility with a kiss be entirely out of line?

His heart swelling with anticipation, he searched her eyes for the answer. Gave her hand an encouraging squeeze.

But to his disappointment, she abruptly looked away. Slipped her hand from his. "Sawyer—"

Hopes doused, he took a step back. "You don't need to say anything, Tori. I understand."

All too well. She'd recently come away from a disappointing relationship. He was not only her employer who was struggling financially, but a former gambler like the parents who'd caused her much heartache, his faith still a wavering question mark. He couldn't blame her for hesitating to take their growing friendship to another level.

"I was only going to say—" she called almost playfully, yet her eyes were anxious as she suddenly turned and started back to Rusty's "—that your carryout is getting cold."

But not as cold as the chill settling into his heart.

He would have kissed her—if she'd let him.

That was one thing Tori was certain of. What she wasn't sure of, though, almost a week later, was why she hadn't let him.

Now, bumping along a narrow forest service road with the boys safely secured in booster seats in the back of Sawyer's crew-cab pickup, she couldn't help glancing at the man whose eyes were steadily focused on the winding dirt road.

As if sensing her attention, he smiled at her. "Don't look so nervous, Tori. This is only a dry run."

He was right. This wasn't a real camping trip, merely a few hours to get the boys accustomed to something more rigorous than the city park.

"I'm not nervous. This will be fun."

But gazing out at the endless ponderosas, she couldn't help but feel uneasy. Should she have run this spur-of-the-moment outing by Ray and Therese first? They'd left that morning for a two-day visit to Tucson to see an MS specialist at the university hospital. When she'd shown up at the Outpost with the boys this afternoon, one thing led to another and the next thing she knew, the twins had talked their big brother into taking them fishing.

It sounded like a good idea at the time, so she'd gone along with it, not wanting to disappoint any of the three Banks brothers. But now that they'd left town, the boys chattering excitedly, she had her doubts. Did that stem from the twins embarking on a miniadventure without consulting their grandparents or was it because things still seemed uncomfortable between Sawyer and her?

They'd had few one-on-one chats when she'd come in to the Outpost on the days she was scheduled to work. Diego or Les always seemed to be around. More customers were putting in an appearance. Conversation remained shallow.

What would they have to say to each other anyway?

She couldn't walk up to him and announce that he'd caught her off guard the evening they'd run into each other at Rusty's. That she'd had time to rethink things— and now how about a do-over?

Was that what she wanted? For Sawyer to kiss her?

She glanced in his direction again, enjoying his back-and-forth with his brothers as they asked questions about fishing. He laughed with them. Teased. Kissing Sawyer would be time well spent; *that* she was sure of. But she needed to establish her quilting business before she could think of being ready for another relationship.

When Heath had pointed her to the door last autumn, he'd insisted it was because she didn't have a life of her own. That she'd put too much of herself into his. Of course, that may have been an excuse to let himself off the hook. She'd heard he'd started dating one of his waitresses shortly thereafter. Maybe he'd had his eye on her for some time and needed a reason to move his faithful fiancée out of the way. But his accusing words had clung to her like superglue.

Was that because there was truth in them?

Had she given up her quilting business too easily? Should she have stood her ground when he'd pooh-poohed it, demanding more and more of her time and energy to get his restaurant launched? Had she used involvement in his business as an excuse to let her own dreams slip away because deep down she feared she couldn't make it work without Grandma?

It was her own fault, though, that Sawyer had assumed cradling his face in her hand signaled she was ready for something more than friendship. But it had only been a gesture of comfort, right?

"Here we go, boys." Sawyer turned off the road and onto an even less used one. Up ahead they could see a small clearing and a good-sized pond. "Kyle assures me it's been restocked with fish."

Clapping from the backseat returned her firmly to the present. She wouldn't let her mixed-up emotions ruin these few hours of fun for the boys. All three of them.

"Now remember what I said." Once they'd parked she held open the back door as Cubby and Landon clambered out. "Stick close. Stay where we can see you. Don't pick up snakes or eat anything with legs."

The boys giggled, as she'd intended.

Sawyer had slathered their exposed skin with sunscreen before they left town. Although it was a moderately warm day in April—midsixties—at this elevation the sun was intense. He'd provided new ball caps, as well. And sunglasses. Both boys were layered with T-shirts, sweaters and windbreakers. Heavy-duty hiking boots.

"Everybody have your fanny packs?" Sawyer unloaded a tackle box and fishing poles, then snagged two pint-size life jackets. "Water? Snacks? Whistles?"

Of course, that reminder set off a chorus of ear-piercing demonstrations, which probably sent wildlife scattering for miles.

"I take that as a yes." He winked at Tori. "Let's go then, guys."

The boys didn't have to be told twice, taking off at breakneck speed toward the pond.

"Boys! Stop!" But they either didn't hear her or didn't intend to obey.

Sawyer let out a shrill whistle that brought them skidding to a halt. When he reached them, he set the gear aside, then squatted. "What did we talk about on the way here?"

"Walk," Cubby admitted, shamefaced. "Don't run."

"And what were you both doing?"

"Running." Landon elbowed Cubby. "But he started it."

"Did not."

"Did, too."

"Uh-uh."

"Whoa." Sawyer T'd his hands. "Time out, fellas. It doesn't matter who started it. We walk out to the water. We don't run. Got it?"

Both nodded.

"Alright, then." Sawyer stood. "Let's go."

Watching the threesome move ahead of her, one twin on each side of their big brother, Tori couldn't help pulling out her cell phone and snapping a photo. That would be a special one to add to Sawyer's memory albums for the boys.

One she might put in hers, as well?

* * *

Sawyer couldn't believe how fast time had flown since they'd arrived midafternoon. Each of the boys had caught a fish—which he had them throw back because he wasn't yet ready to teach them how to clean one—but there had also been time for a short hike and animal-tracking lessons. Deer. Elk. Javelina.

Yet all the while, he'd been acutely aware of Tori's presence. Watching for her smile. Listening for her laugh. Enjoying her interactions with Cubby and Landon. Delighting in the instances when his eye caught hers and they'd silently shared a laugh at something one of the youngsters had said or done.

Although it had been almost a week since he'd foolishly misinterpreted her comforting gesture and gotten ahead of himself, he still sensed she wasn't entirely at ease when he was around and had put some distance between them. Which was what made her agreeing to this outing today doubly appreciated. For the boys' sakes, of course.

"So is anybody hungry?"

His question was met with a round of raised hands, Tori's waving the hardest. With the late-afternoon sun just dipping behind the tops of the ponderosa pines, he gave the boys a lesson in fire building, then they roasted turkey hot dogs and finished up with marshmallows and a lot of laughter.

It had been a good day.

Now loading up the truck, they'd get home before dark.

"I'm glad you had us bring gloves." Tori rubbed her hands up and down her jacketed arms, glancing back at the twins, who were vigorously stirring the doused campfire into a muddy mess. Shoveling on dirt with a little hand shovel. Pouring on water. Stirring, stirring, stirring.

"At this elevation it gets nippy fast when the sun goes behind the trees, doesn't it?" He lifted the insulated cooler into the bed of the pickup.

"It does. It's probably at least ten or fifteen degrees warmer in Jerome right now, if not more."

"Having second thoughts about relocating to mountain country?"

"Absolutely not."

For some reason, it made him glad to know that. They chatted for several more minutes as he secured their gear. As the afternoon had progressed, the tension between them eased and they seemed to be falling back into their earlier comfort zone.

He looked over his shoulder. "Hey, Landon. Where's the Cubster? We're ready to go."

"He had to go to the bathroom."

Tori's forehead creased. "I hope he doesn't encounter anything poisonous. I don't know how I'd explain that to Ray and Therese."

"I didn't see anything like that right around here when we were hiking, so while he might get chilled taking care of business, he'll be okay." He double-checked the fishing rods to make sure they were fastened down. "But you're concerned that we took the boys out for a few hours without express permission from their grandparents, aren't you?"

"Well…"

"Tori, they okayed an overnighter already. You've been at the house for almost two months now. They trust your judgment."

"I know, but—"

"Enough." With a grin, he touched his finger briefly to the tip of her nose. "It's all good."

She nodded, her smile admitting he was right.

"Ready to roll, boys?" He glanced around as he strolled to the giant mud pie to double-check that the fire was out. Landon was standing off to the side, zipping his jacket. "Where's your brother?"

"I told you. He went to the bathroom."

"Still?"

Landon shrugged.

Sawyer put his hands to his mouth, megaphone style. "Cubby! Finish up your business. We're ready to go home."

Tori looked at him uncertainly. "He stuffed himself on marshmallows. I hope he didn't make himself sick."

"Naw. Banks boys are tough." But he could tell Tori didn't like the thought of the little guy overindulging and her having to explain *that* to Ray and Therese. He took a few steps away and again called to his brother. "Cub! Can you hear me?"

No response.

"Guess I'd better check on him." He turned to Landon, who was climbing into the backseat of the truck. "Which way did your brother go?"

Landon shrugged.

"He didn't go near the water, did he?" Sawyer's gaze raked the pond's perimeter.

"How would I know?"

The old Bible story words "am I my brother's keeper?" came to mind. "I'll be back, Tori. Hop on in the truck to keep warm."

He handed her his keys.

He'd been over outdoor safety with the boys repeatedly. *If you get lost, don't wander around. Stay in one place. Use your whistle.* He hadn't heard the piercing signal yet, so Cubby must be nearby, just out of view.

Heading for the stand of trees closest to where they'd had the fire and enjoyed their supper, he called out again, then paused to listen. But the forest remained silent. A whisper of apprehension prickled at the back of his neck as he moved in among the pines. The youngster wouldn't have gone far. Just far enough to where he thought he'd have some privacy, right?

But fifteen minutes later, having walked along the woodland path encircling the pond, he still saw no sign of Cubby. No response to Sawyer's repeated calls.

As he stepped into the clearing not too far from the truck, Tori joined him, fear in her eyes. "Why doesn't he come when you call? Or blow his whistle?"

Sawyer didn't have an answer to that. "Maybe he wandered out of earshot."

"So what do we do? Split up to search?"

"I don't want you and Landon lost in the woods, too."

She gripped his arm. "You think he's lost."

He needed to be more careful of his words. "He can't have gotten far. But it would be better if you both stay here. That way when he shows up, he won't be scared that he's been left alone and set out again to look for us."

"It'll be dark soon, Sawyer."

The sun, while still filtering through the thick, endless stretches of pine, was low in the sky. The forest was becoming shadowed. He slipped his arm around her, surprised that she was trembling. He pulled her close. "Nothing to be scared about. He knows what to do if he loses his bearings. He has his fanny pack with water and snacks. A flashlight."

But what if he'd gotten himself turned around and panicked? Started running in the wrong direction. Or had fallen. Hit his head and didn't respond to his big brother's cries because he was incapable of hearing them. Or what if he'd gone back to the pond without his life jacket when no one was looking?

"God knows right where he is." Tori's soft voice held a determined edge. "I'm praying He'll find him for us. Soon."

She was welcome to do all the praying she wanted. But right now, he wasn't about to sit back and rely on a God who'd let him down one too many times.

"You have your cell phone, right? I'll call when I locate him." He nodded to his vehicle. "Get back in the truck to stay warm. Honk if Cubby shows up here first."

Reluctant to release her, he nevertheless gave her a hug before once again moving in among the trees.

Come on, Jacob Anderson Banks. Use that whistle.

Checking his watch, he hiked in considerably deeper, noting nature's markers as he went. A pine trunk long ago split by lightning. An outcropping of rock. A fallen, rotting log.

As the sun rays filtered through the needled branches, he covered uneven ground thickly layered in brown pine needles, pinecones crunching under his boots. He'd thought he'd been keeping a close eye on the boys, but obviously he'd messed up.

Just like he'd done with Vanessa and Dad's water heater.

He called again for Cubby, pausing to listen.

Nothing.

Fisting his fingers, he plunged on through the trees, superstitiously biting back the prayer forming on his lips. He dared not voice a plea. He couldn't bring himself to do it. His track record for that was none too good.

He glanced again at his watch, startled to see another

thirty minutes had passed. No sound of the truck's horn. It would be dark soon. Tori would be worrying herself sick.

Cub might be around the next rocky outcropping, but he couldn't wait any longer to call the county sheriff's office. His search-and-rescue buddies needed to be brought in. He pulled out his cell phone.

Then his heart sank. No bars.

He'd been out here many times before. Always had a signal.

What was he supposed to do now? Get Tori to drive back to town for help while he kept searching?

He swallowed hard. Then, with only a moment's hesitation, he dropped to his knees on the forest floor. Lifted his gaze to the fading light above. He no longer had a choice. He had to risk it.

"Father God…" His words came softly. "I know it's been a while since You've heard from me and I'm not going to make any excuses for that. You understand the whys of it better than anyone."

High up in one of the trees, a squirrel's claws skittered as it scampered from limb to limb. But Sawyer paid it no mind.

"Tori says You know where my little brother is. That You can find him for us. I'd sure like to believe that."

He cleared his throat. "You know how hard it is for me to ask. I've been on my knees before. For Mom. Then Dad and Vanessa. I feel almost as if by asking…that I'm signing my Cubster's death warrant."

How ungrateful that sounded. But he couldn't be anything but honest. He raised his voice.

"I'm going to trust You here. Lay it on the line. I've messed up. Again. But I need to find Cubby. And soon. *Please?* For Tori, if not for me."

She'd blame herself for not having asked permission from Ray and Therese to take them out for an afternoon adventure.

Some adventure.

But it wasn't her fault. The blame lay solidly on his doorstep.

He remained on his knees, watching the tops of the pines sway slightly in the higher-up breeze.

"I know You're not into bargaining. Bartering. Making deals. I tried that one too many times. But I'll tell You this and You can take it or leave it as You see fit…if You'll point me in the right direction, let me bring Cubby back safe and sound…well, I'll owe You. Big-time."

But no inner promptings or audible voice from Heaven pointed him the direction he needed to go. With a heavy heart, he got to his feet, his mind now trudging through the sludge of disappointment as he attempted to focus on his best options to get a search-and-rescue team out here as fast as possible.

If God wasn't willing to help, then he'd find his little brother on his own if it was the last thing he ever did.

Drawing a deep breath, he turned back in the direction he'd come just as, in the distance, his truck's horn blared.

Chapter Fourteen

Tori had never been happier to see anyone as when Sawyer emerged from the surrounding forest—except for a short while ago when a couple of young hikers had walked into the clearing with Cubby beside them.

Fighting tears, her heart filled with joy, she'd hugged the boy close, then immediately sounded the truck horn long and hard.

She met Sawyer when he was halfway to the truck, his gaze locked on Cubby and Landon and the couple who'd come to the little boy's rescue.

She wanted to throw her arms around Sawyer. To cry with relief. But she held herself back.

"Julie Rollins and Matt Bell—they live in Hunter Ridge—were hiking and found Cubby. He told them we'd been at the pond fishing and they knew right where that was."

Relief momentarily flooded Sawyer's eyes, then his expression hardened. "When I get my hands on that kid—"

"Sawyer." She touched his arm. Now that she had Cubby safely back, she hadn't the heart to scold him for wandering off. There would be time enough for that later.

"Not right now. Not in front of his brother or his rescuers. And not in anger. Please?"

Something seemed to war within him, and for a moment she thought he'd push right by her and call his little brother on the carpet. But he gave a brisk nod and together they approached the waiting group. Without a word, he gathered Cubby into a hug, then shook the hands of Julie and Matt, who modestly claimed they'd merely been in the right place at the right time.

On the return to town, Tori chatted quietly with the boys, but Sawyer remained mostly silent, only speaking when spoken to. They arrived at the house not long after dark and she herded the twins inside to get cleaned up while Sawyer appeared preoccupied with reorganizing his gear in the back of the truck.

She paused in the doorway to call to him. "Come in when you're finished there."

He didn't respond immediately and for a moment she thought he hadn't heard her. "Sawyer? Come in when—"

"We'll see."

Maybe it was just as well that he stayed away. She intended to get the boys cleaned up and tucked into bed. Then tomorrow morning she and Cubby would have a long talk before his grandparents came back that night. Right now she wanted only to treasure the boy's safe return and have the day end in peace.

Which was unlikely to happen if Sawyer joined them.

She planned to let the boys share the guest bedroom, unwilling tonight to shuffle them off to isolation in their separate spaces. Bath and story time were followed by prayers, but she remained on high alert, listening for the sound of the front door closing or the creak of a stair. Once she thought she heard the squeak of a floorboard, but to her relief the bedtime rituals were uninterrupted.

So when she turned out the light, pulled the door closed behind her and started down the hallway, she was startled to see Sawyer sitting, sock-footed, on the floor not far from the top of the staircase. His back was against the wall, arms folded on bent knees. Head down.

He looked up as she approached, then rose slowly to his feet. "All tucked in?"

"Two tired boys."

He nodded, his voice low. "A little too much adventure for all of us."

She motioned for him to follow her down the stairs to the parlor, where she kicked off her shoes, sat down on the love seat and tucked her feet under her. He lowered himself to a chair that was way too small for a man his size, then stretched out his legs.

"Thank you, Sawyer, for letting me handle things the way I think they should be handled. I'll be talking to Cubby in the morning."

"He took about fifty years off my life."

"Mine, too."

He held her gaze. "None of this was your fault, Tori. I take entire responsibility."

"No. I'm responsible, as well. I should have been keeping a closer eye on them." Not been paying so much attention to Sawyer.

"Did he give any explanation? Any excuse for what he did? Why didn't he sit still and blow his whistle like I told him to do if he got lost?"

"Because he wasn't lost."

Sawyer raised a brow. "Come again?"

"You'd told the boys to use the whistle if they got lost. He said he wasn't lost. He was tracking a deer."

"A deer."

"Remember? You showed the boys how to tell the

difference between deer and elk tracks. He found a deer track. Then he apparently got preoccupied, and must have gotten too far out. Couldn't hear us calling for him."

Sawyer released a pent-up breath. "We told them both to stay where we could see them."

"I know. But he's not even five years old yet. Kids forget. He wasn't trying to be bad."

"You realize, don't you, that this could have had a whole different ending if that couple hadn't come across him? I was ready to call the sheriff's department, get a search-and-rescue team out there before it totally got dark. If Matt and Julie hadn't been good and decent people…"

Tears pricked her eyes as she uncurled herself from the sofa and stood to look down at him. "You're not telling me anything I don't know."

Sawyer was immediately on his feet, reaching for her just as she neared the door to the front entryway. "I'm sorry, Tori. I didn't mean—"

"I know. It's just that—" Her voice cracked.

He put his arms around her and pulled her close in a comforting hug. "We've had a scare today."

She slipped her arms around his waist, nodding against the solidness of his chest. "One I hope never to have again."

"Me, too." He continued to hold her, both lost in their own relief-filled thoughts. "I'm wondering…you know, if taking them on a camping trip is that great of an idea now. Maybe we should wait until they're older. You know, like twenty-one."

She couldn't help but giggle. "Let's not punish them for this. While we haven't established a date yet, they know their grandparents agreed to the outing. They'd be disappointed if the trip got canceled."

"But what's the alternative? Put leashes on them? They're too big for playpens."

A faint smile surfacing, she plucked at his shirtfront, knowing he was doing his best to ward off her tears. She probably wouldn't sleep a wink tonight once the what-ifs slammed into her full force, but right now, with Sawyer's strong arms around her, the fear that had taken hold during that afternoon's longest hour of her life eased a fraction more.

"Do you think," she suggested, "that they make those baby sling carriers big enough for forty-pounders?"

She felt his chest silently rumble with laughter as he no doubt pictured each of them staggering along a trail with a twin looped in a sling. "Now, there's an idea."

They were silent, the minutes ticking by to the sound of the old grandfather clock in the corner. Then she whispered, "I was praying so hard, Sawyer."

His arms tightened around her. "Me, too."

She pulled slightly back to look up at him. "God answered your prayers this time."

Sawyer's jaw hardened and he gave a quick nod. "He did."

"So you can't say anymore that He doesn't listen to you."

Something flickered through his eyes as their gazes locked. He swallowed. "No. No, I can't."

Then her breath caught as she realized he was lowering his mouth to hers.

Sweet. All sweet. He moved his mouth gently against the inviting softness of Tori's. Was this another answered prayer? Being allowed to hold her like this? Feeling her snuggle more deeply into his arms as if she'd always belonged there?

He heard her soft sigh and deepened the kiss.

Tori. Who would have thought on that snowy February day when he'd interviewed her as a possible caregiver for his brothers that they'd wind up *here*? Locked in each other's arms. And it feeling so *right*.

No, he wasn't in any better position in this moment to get involved with a woman than he had been yesterday. But this wasn't just any woman. This was Tori. His sweet, sweet Tori.

When he drew back, she opened her eyes and they continued to gaze at each other. Content to remain in the warmth of the other's embrace.

"Wow." Her voice was barely an audible breath.

"I couldn't have worded it better." In fact, he couldn't have worded it at all. He'd never felt this way before. How could he put into words the most amazing moment of his life? But surely she could guess. Could feel the thundering pound of his heart beneath the hand she'd pressed to his chest.

She shifted slightly in his arms.

"I'm not good with words, Tori," he said suddenly, sensing she might be ready to step away. He'd do about anything to keep her right where she was. Cuddled up close to his heart. Forever. "But you need to know…"

Know what? That his heart nearly pounded right out of his chest when she looked at him? That he loved how one corner of her mouth turned up kind of crookedly when she smiled? Loved how she related to his brothers. That he was determined to find a way to convince her that *he* was everything she'd ever want or need in a man.

"Know what?" she echoed, her eyes searching his.

His brain went blank, his mouth suddenly dry. All he could do was lean in for another sweet kiss. And when some moments later he drew back, he smiled down at her dazed expression. "I'm hoping that says it all."

"Tori?" From the top of the stairs the voice of one of the twins—Cubby?—called down. He must have seen the light on below. "We think there's a mouse in our room."

Looking somewhat disoriented and thoroughly kissed, Tori pulled away, alarmed eyes meeting his. "A mouse? I think that's your department, isn't it?"

Feeling befuddled himself, he nodded. "Do you know where Ray keeps the traps?"

"Garage probably."

"I'm on it."

As Tori hurried up the stairs to reassure the twins, he pulled on his boots and headed out to the detached garage, drinking in the cold night air almost like a man who'd been held under water for a too-long time.

What had just happened in there?

If the grin tugging at his lips was any indication, something mighty unexpected. And better than anything he could have dreamed up.

He located the traps in short order, paused in the kitchen to snag a few chunks of cheese and joined Tori upstairs. She was ushering the twins out of one room and into two others.

He pulled her aside. "What's the deal with separate rooms?"

"I let them stay in the guest room's big double bed tonight rather than in their single beds in their own rooms," she said quietly, "thinking that maybe after what happened today they'd appreciate each other's company."

"They don't share a room? They used to, didn't they? At least they did when they lived with their mom and dad. I remember them whispering and giggling together long after lights-out."

"They shared here, too, until recently. But when Cubby had his upset a few weeks ago, missing his parents, Ray felt it best to separate them."

"What good is isolating them supposed to do? That could make him feel worse."

"I let Ray know how I felt about it, too. But he was adamant." She nodded to the mousetraps. "The coast is clear in the guest room now if you want to take care of that."

There were other things he'd like to say about Ray's decision to separate the boys, but it sounded as if he and Tori were on the same page with this. He was glad that she'd spoken up.

He made quick work laying the traps, then stepped again into the hallway as she was closing one of the bedroom doors. The other one was already closed.

"They'll be okay?"

"They're doing fine. It was silly me that decided they needed to be together tonight."

"That's not silly. It's smart. Makes sense."

He sure didn't look forward to heading out to his cabin and lying awake alone with his thoughts. What a day. Between Cubby's close call and the kiss he'd shared with Tori, he'd toss and turn all night.

She walked him down the stairs to the front door, where they stood awkwardly. Dare he try to steal a parting kiss? Or would she rebuff him, thinking there had been enough of that for one night?

"I guess I'll be seeing you later, then," he offered in his most gentlemanly tones.

To his surprise, she stepped forward to touch her lips to his. He didn't need any further coaxing and matched her kiss for kiss.

When with a laugh she finally pushed him out the door, it took a moment for him to orient himself to where he'd parked his truck. He grinned as he slid in behind the steering wheel. Man, that gal could kiss.

He could get used to this.

Tori flipped the dead bolt on the front door, then leaned back against it.

Sawyer had kissed her.

She'd kissed him back.

I'm hoping that says it all.

That's what he'd said at the conclusion of one of his mind-blowing kisses. But what was he really *saying*? Stating a fact that he enjoyed kissing…or something more?

She closed her eyes. "What have I gotten myself into, Lord?"

Surely Sawyer didn't mean what it sounded as if he meant. That he was interested in her. Wanted to see more of her. Wanted…what? A future together? She was no outdoorswoman. Her professional interests lay elsewhere. She was the paid childcare giver, not him, but she'd lost track of his precious little brother. Yet he hadn't blamed her. Claimed responsibility himself.

"Please bless Cubby's rescuers," she murmured, her heart overflowing with thankfulness, "for bringing him back safely. And thank You for answering Sawyer's and my prayers. For showing him You *do* listen. That You *do* care."

She stood there for some time, a thankful heart reviewing the events of the day. Not surprisingly, her thoughts eventually made their way back to Sawyer. His kisses. His intriguing words.

"Please, my Heavenly Father, let me not rush ahead of You and strike out on a road You don't want me taking. I don't want to be like Cubby, moving excitedly into territory where I have no business being, not realizing I'm lost until You have to come find me."

In the quietness of the night, a peace settled in her heart. A reassurance that together she and God would take one step at a time.

And yet…a tiny voice nagged in the corner of her mind.

Had Sawyer's kisses been driven by nothing more than relief? The aftermath of their shared fear for his little brother's safety?

Chapter Fifteen

Sawyer didn't miss the surprised looks on a few folks' faces—or Kyle's big grin—when he slipped into the pew next to Tori and the boys on Sunday morning. Ray, on the other side of the twins and next to Therese, seemed downright flabbergasted.

But all he cared about was the happy look in Tori's eyes—and the assurance in his heart that God welcomed him here. The Lord had come through for him in rescuing his Cub. The least he could do in appreciation was to show the world whose team he was fully on now.

During Pastor McCrae's morning message, Sawyer couldn't help but surreptitiously steal his hand over to clasp Tori's. She didn't pull away, and if he wasn't mistaken, her cheeks flushed rosier than usual. He could only hope, though, that those around them couldn't hear his heart thrumming when she gave his hand a gentle squeeze before releasing it as they stood for the closing song.

After the service, Cubby and Landon followed him into the aisle.

Cubby grasped his hand and looked up at him with hope-filled eyes. "Can I go home with you?"

Where had that come from? He'd never had the boys out to his cabin, but the mere thought of them romping around out there tugged at Sawyer's heartstrings. "Not today, buddy."

"When?"

He caught Ray's frown. "Well, sometime."

"When?"

He and Tori had filled the Selbys in on the fishing trip events that had transpired only a few days ago. Playing down, of course, the length of time Cubby had gone missing and the terror that had laced their hearts. For Cubby and Landon's part, they didn't seem the least bit fazed by the close call. Cubby hadn't yet fully grasped that he *had* been lost. But Sawyer suspected Ray was rethinking the camping trip and he didn't need any other mishaps with the boys weighing in on that decision.

Ignoring Ray, Sawyer squatted down by his brother. "I'm fixing things up at my cabin. There are sharp tools and equipment, so it's not a good place for little boys right now."

Landon bumped his brother out of the way. "Maybe we can live with you when you're done. You know, when you marry Tori."

Stunned, he looked up into Tori's equally astonished face. Behind her, Ray didn't look any too thrilled either.

"Hey, bud." He kept his voice casual. "Who told you Tori and I are getting married?"

He cringed. His wording made it sound like a confirmation, as if it were a fact.

Landon's face scrunched. "Cubby said you kissed her."

A wave of heat rushed up his neck. Had Cubby come clear down the stairs the other night, or far enough down that he could see them in the parlor doorway, before scurrying back to the top to call down to them? Or had he peeked down later to spy Tori giving his big brother that amazing send-off at the door?

"Just because someone kisses someone, it doesn't mean they're going to get married." *Careful here, Banks. Don't dig yourself in too deep.*

Cubby pushed in front of his brother. "But we want you to. We decided. Then we can move to your house."

How was he going to get out of this one? If he said they weren't getting married, what message would that send to the woman standing beside him? They hadn't talked about anything of that nature since the evening after they'd lost Cubby. He hadn't ruled it out, that was for sure. But they weren't anywhere near there yet.

Would the boys interpret his words as if it were okay to kiss any pretty woman you wanted to, whenever you wanted to, commitment-free? He'd have his hands full when they were teens if that's the lesson that got lodged in their heads.

"Believe me, guys, you don't want to move into my house. My...my dogs are stinky." His pinched his fingers to his nose. "They need a bath."

Cubby's eyes widened. "You have dogs? More than one? And room for a pony?"

"One for each of us?" Landon shot his twin a look that said their older brother's house was the answer to their dreams.

Think fast.

"You like to eat, though, don't you?"

Both bobbed their heads.

He looked at them sadly. "I'm sorry, but I can't cook."

Two pairs of eyes turned confidently in Tori's direction as they spoke in unison. "*She* can."

Was it his imagination, or were the people around them lingering longer than necessary? Listening in on the minidrama—or was it a comedy?—unfolding right under their noses.

"Boys!" Ray's voice, low but firm, captured the attention of his grandsons. "It's time for lunch now. Let's go."

"But—"

"No buts." He jerked his head toward the door. "Your grandma is going to fix fried chicken and mashed potatoes, so let's not keep her waiting."

"I imagine there will be green beans, too," Sawyer encouraged as he stood again, the disappointed looks on his brothers' upturned faces breaking his heart. But what could he do? He was in no position to take the boys in, even if Therese and Ray were on board with it. And they most certainly were not.

And what did the Selbys think of the fact that he and Tori had carelessly allowed one of the twins to see them sharing a kiss? Or two.

As Ray ushered the boys down the aisle, Sawyer got up the gumption to turn to Tori, fearful of what he might see in her beautiful eyes. Who would have thought the boys would boldly announce their kiss to the world? And in *church* of all places!

Just because someone kisses someone, it doesn't mean they're going to get married.

She knew that. It didn't come as any surprise. But Sawyer's words served to remind her that they were a long way off from making any commitments.

His gaze met hers in apology. "I'm sorry about that."

"It's not your fault," she said softly, mindful of those

around them as they headed out a side door, then into the parking lot. "I had no idea Cubby had seen us."

"Me neither. But somehow I need to clarify to Ray and Therese that's *all* Cubby would have seen. He didn't stumble onto some hot-and-heavy make-out session."

Her face warmed. Would the Selbys jump to conclusions and assume that's what she and Sawyer had been up to when they'd misplaced Cubby on the fishing trip?

"I also hope," Sawyer continued, "that they don't think I've been planting seeds of discontent. The boys have never been out to my place. I've never so much as hinted that they come visit me, let alone move in with me."

"I can confirm that, Sawyer. You've never been with them but when I've been with you, too."

He nodded in the direction of her car, and together they walked to it. He opened the door and she slipped in behind the steering wheel.

"I want to apologize, Tori, that on top of the fishing trip fiasco, the boys have further put you in an awkward position with your employers because of what Cubby saw."

"I'll talk to them. Get things smoothed over." If she could.

"Again. I'm sorry. But—" he leaned in slightly "—I still don't regret that kiss. I hope you don't either."

And with that parting line, to which she had no chance to respond, he shut the door and headed to his pickup. She sat there for a long moment digesting his words. He didn't regret the kiss. But seeing how it had confused the twins and complicated her relationship with the Selbys, did she?

She didn't have much time to think about it as she headed straight home to change clothes and step in to help Therese with lunch preparations. It was only after mealtime when Ray had taken the boys on a walk that she had privacy to speak with Therese.

Loading the last of the pots and pans in the dishwasher, she quickly evaluated her friend's mood and energy level. Both had been even keel throughout the meal. "Do you have a few minutes to chat, Therese, before Ray and the twins get back?"

Therese moved to the cleared kitchen table and pulled out a chair. Tori did likewise. How do you broach a subject like the one she needed to engage in? Jumping in feetfirst appeared to be the best way.

"I know you heard Landon say that Cubby saw Sawyer kissing me."

The older woman gave a thin smile as she clasped her hands on the table. Nothing more. She wasn't going to make this easy.

"I want you to know that nothing like that had ever happened before. Not until the evening after we got Cubby safely home. We—I think we were both so relieved, thankful that nothing more serious had happened, that we let our guards down. Sought reassurance. Comfort."

"I see."

"I want you to know there was nothing improper about it. Nothing happened beyond a kiss."

Or rather several kisses, but that was immaterial to this conversation.

Therese's clasped hands tightened. "Thank you for sharing that with me. While Ray and I sensed some mutual interest there, we hadn't realized…you know, that the two of you were becoming quite so close. Then when the boys started talking marriage and moving in with the two of you—"

"That's entirely in their imaginations," Tori was quick to clarify. "It's only been a few days since Cubby got lost. I've had no further communication with Sawyer since then. Not until church this morning. So there's been no talk of marriage or anything in the least bit futuristic."

Therese seemed to relax somewhat.

"I also want you to know," Tori hurried on, needing to clear the air completely, "that Sawyer has had no contact with the boys except when I've been there with him. You have my word that in no way, shape or form has he alluded to the twins that they should move in with him. Or us. That's entirely their fabrication based on what Cubby thought he saw."

"What he *did* see, you mean."

Tori drew a breath. "Yes."

"Well, I do thank you for being open with me, Tori. This eases my mind and I know it will Ray's, as well. We know that we're not as young and dynamic or as *fun* as you and Sawyer in the boys' eyes. But we do love them and we want them to be happy. It's unsettling that suddenly we're hearing them voicing an eagerness to move in with the two of you. To leave us in the dust."

Tori reached out to cover the older woman's hands still clasped on the table. "They don't want to leave you in the dust. They're four and a half years old. They don't know what they want, except what seems most shiny at any given moment. Five minutes later that can change."

Therese cracked a smile. "That is true, isn't it?"

"It is. So please, Therese, don't take to heart anything like that. I've been here long enough to know those two little guys love you and Ray to pieces. That you've created for them a safe, secure and happy home."

"Thank you. I needed to hear that."

"I'd be more than happy to repeat it anytime you'd like me to."

Therese squeezed her hand. "You're a dear young woman, Tori. You've been such a blessing since you've joined our family."

"And I needed to hear *that*, too." She'd been worried the past few days with all that had happened on the fishing trip that the Selbys might be having second thoughts about bringing her into their home. And now this kissing business…

"While we're here, Tori…" An uncertainty flickered through Therese's eyes, and Tori tensed. "It's probably none of my business, and you can tell me so and it won't hurt my feelings in the least. Maybe I'm being an old busybody."

A wave of uneasiness washed through her, but she smiled anyway. "What's up?"

"You said not long ago that you'd come out of a disappointing relationship."

"I did."

"You've come to mean so much to me in such a short time. I don't want you to be disappointed again."

"You mean, with Sawyer?"

"Yes."

"Therese, I need you to be honest with me. I've picked up on something that I can only describe as tension between Ray and Sawyer. You yourself alluded in the past that Sawyer might not be who I think he is. I need to know what it is that concerns you about him—and me."

Were they aware of his gambling past? Had they reason to believe that wasn't over after all, as he'd led her to believe? That more recent gambling impacted the many bills he was currently paying off?

Therese remained silent.

"Is it fair," Tori prompted, "to withhold from me something I may possibly be getting myself into? Has he done something illegal? Immoral?"

Therese sat back, her eyes rounding. "Oh, dear me. Nothing of that nature. Not to my knowledge anyway."

"Then what?"

"Oh, sweetie…" Therese sighed. "Sawyer is a bright, ambitious and charming young man."

"And *that's* why you think I should steer clear of him?"

"No, I mean that on the surface he looks like every young woman's dream."

"But you're saying he isn't."

"I've come to care for you, as has Ray. We'd like to see you with a young man who can be counted on. One who hangs in there when the going gets tough. Believe me, there's probably not a marriage in existence, including those proverbial matches made in Heaven, where times haven't gotten tough."

"What makes you think he's not that kind of man?"

Therese studied her thoughtfully. "When my daughter gave birth to the twins, Sawyer was one proud big brother. Not as we would have guessed at all. We thought he might resent his dad starting a second family. But not Sawyer. He was over at their place at every opportunity, gamely changing diapers and giving Mama and Papa a break whenever they needed one. Vanessa used to get tickled at how he doted on the boys."

"And then?"

"When my daughter…" She paused, blinked back

tears. "When Vanessa and Anderson were killed, we fully expected Sawyer would continue to be involved in his brothers' lives. After all, he was a legal backup should something happen to Ray and me. We thought his presence would lend stability. But he didn't come through. In fact, for a time he disappeared out of their lives altogether."

"Wouldn't that be understandable? I mean, the boys' father is his father, too. He was grieving, as well."

"That's what we initially assumed, so later we reached out to him and were delighted that he again made an effort. The boys took to him like you wouldn't believe. Looked forward to his visits. Stuck to him like glue every time he'd pop over."

"What happened?"

"I don't know. But after a few weeks he stopped coming around. It was nearing the anniversary of his father's death. Maybe that had something to do with it. But the boys were brokenhearted, asking about him all the time. They'd both run straight to Sawyer when we'd encounter him around town. He always acted as if he was happy to see them, but he didn't come to the house anymore."

"I don't think it's because he didn't care." She *knew* he cared.

"Gradually Cubby and Landon got used to him not being there. And then—" she smiled at Tori "—you joined our household and on your first day here, up pops Sawyer. Out of the blue. Once again the twins are becoming attached to him. Now they're even saying they want to move in with him. He's making an effort to take them fishing. Making promises about a camping trip. But—"

Therese looked at her helplessly, as if reluctant to continue.

"Go on, please."

"Quite honestly? I don't trust that to last, Tori. He'll tire of it and move on again. The boys will get hurt. And for that reason, I'm not sure how long your relationship would last with him either, not if his track record when it comes to commitment is any indication."

A leaden weight settled into Tori's stomach.

"I'm not trying to discourage you if you have an interest in Sawyer. He's a fine young man in so many ways. But Ray and I've learned to be cautious, for the boys' sake." She patted Tori's hand. "I care for you, and I want you to go into any relationship with Sawyer with your eyes wide-open."

Numb, Tori stood and leaned over to give her friend a hug. "Thank you, Therese."

It was special to have an older woman in her life again. One who cared about her. She missed her grandmother. But what Therese shared with her out of love was troubling.

Was her friend right about Sawyer?

Sawyer blinked. Rubbed his eyes. Looked at the numbers on the electronic spreadsheet again.

May was almost here, but the busiest part of the season wouldn't get started until closer to Memorial Day weekend. Yet his profits had taken an unexpected upswing. Another month of this and he might be able to double up on payments owed to Kyle and Graham. Get them paid off sooner than expected.

He hadn't seen that coming.

Pushing back in his office chair, he squinted one eye and looked Heavenward. "Guess I have You to thank for this, huh?"

Normally he'd be patting himself on the back right about now, congratulating himself on cutting costs and doing a better job of selecting and displaying merchandise. Investing in good advertising. But it was clear those efforts wouldn't have amounted to a hill of beans if God hadn't decided to bless them.

He hadn't had any unexpected expenses either. The truck was holding up. The cabin roof hadn't leaked. Nothing had worn out or prematurely fallen apart at the Outpost over the winter. A big turnaround from the previous year.

Which meant he *might* be in a much better position to court Tori Janner than he'd originally thought. *Court.* He chuckled at the old-fashioned word. But that's how Tori made him feel. Old-fashioned in the good sense of the word. Gallant. Gentlemanly. Chivalrous.

He longed to be her knight in shining armor. Her hero. Her husband?

He said the word aloud, savoring it on his tongue. Liking the sound of it.

"What do You think of that?" he shot Heavenward again, suddenly glad it was late at night, long after the store had been locked up and no one was around to think he was having a heart-to-heart with his ceiling.

Did other men kiss a woman once and then out of the blue contemplate getting married? That was pretty crazy stuff, he had to admit. No doubt Tori wasn't anywhere near that kind of thinking. So a courtship was in order.

And a big dollop of God's paving the way.

And yet…marriage. Starting a family. That was a huge leap for both of them.

He abruptly stood to pace the floor of his office, the wooden floorboards creaking under his booted feet.

While she hadn't objected to his kisses, with Tori's family background, would she welcome the courtship of a former gambler? She didn't yet know about his involvement in the deaths of the twins' parents either. If he were advising a female friend about a guy like him, he'd have serious reservations. Caution her.

And what about him? As tempting as it was to focus on the promising aspects of a relationship with an amazing woman like Tori, was he really capable of making a lifetime commitment?

Chapter Sixteen

"You must be Tori Janner. I've heard so many good things about you."

Standing inside the front door of the Selbys' home a few days later, Tori stared up at a distinguished-looking man who appeared to be in his late forties. Dressed casually in dark gray trousers, a navy golf shirt and black oxfords, he looked vaguely familiar.

"Pastor Curtis Selby." He thrust out his hand to shake hers. "Therese and Ray's eldest."

Pastor? No one mentioned that before. And neither of her employers had said anything about expecting company.

"And this," he continued, stepping aside and motioning to a dark-haired woman coming up the porch steps, "is my better half, Fay."

She shook hands with his wife, then stepped back. "Please come in. I'll let your parents know you're here, Pastor."

"Curtis or Curt will do." He smiled widely, and at last recognizing the resemblance to his father, she immediately liked him. He lowered his voice conspiratorially.

"This was a spur-of-the-moment trip, so let me announce myself. Surprise them."

They'd be surprised, alright.

"They're in the kitchen."

Fay gave Tori a good-natured smile, then followed her husband past the staircase and to the rear of the house.

As she closed the front door, Tori could hear the welcoming roar of the men and squeals of laughter from the women coming from the kitchen. A spur-of-the-moment visit. She'd never, herself, been one for drop-in guests, but a son and daughter-in-law driving from California might truly be a delightful occasion. So why did she feel uneasy about it?

She didn't have long to wait to find out.

"Curtis is here to talk some sense into us," Therese confided, her voice low, as Tori helped her throw together a quick lunch. "Say a prayer that I don't crown him with a frying pan."

"He drove over here for that? Instead of a phone call?"

"Oh, there's more. His two brothers and their wives will be here shortly."

"You're kidding."

"Unfortunately, no." She looked around the room somewhat helplessly. "I hate it when I have to ask you to do things outside of taking care of the boys. Ray and I'll sleep on the sofa bed in the library tonight. But after lunch if you could make sure the guest room is ready and move one of the boys to free up another room for a rollaway, I'd be eternally grateful."

"I'd be happy to."

From the dining room, she could hear Fay and Curtis chatting with the kids and Ray. Hear the twins' giggles.

"So, what exactly does 'talking sense into you' mean?"

"Relocating to California."

"Taking the boys with you?"

"Moving with or without the twins isn't even under consideration on our part. We have no plans to leave Hunter Ridge. They mean well, but we've been through these discussions repeatedly with our sons ever since we first retired. When Vanessa checked in on us regularly, they didn't fight us too hard. But after she passed away and we took in the twins, well, it's been a different story."

She gave Tori's arm a squeeze. "But don't you worry. We're not going anywhere and you'll still have a job."

While concerning, keeping her job was the least of her worries. The boys being taken from Hunter Ridge right when Sawyer was beginning to rebond with them was another story.

Invited to join the family for lunch, Tori couldn't think of a polite way to decline. Therese insisted she wanted her son to get to know the remarkable woman who cared for their grandsons. To reassure him that there was nothing for him to concern himself with.

It turned out to be a pleasant lunch, with the boys on their best behavior and the conversation relaxed and not touching on any sensitive subjects—like relocation to the Golden State. They'd barely finished eating when the doorbell rang and Tori excused herself to answer it. Two more sons and their spouses greeted her, looking her over curiously as if wondering how one so young could possibly be handling their sister's children expertly enough to relieve their parents of the bulk of childcare responsibilities.

She fixed a few more sandwiches for the newcomers. Opened another bag of chips. Then she headed off to the Outpost for the afternoon, apprehension regarding the outcome of the Selby children's visit weighing heavily.

And wouldn't you know it. Les and Diego weren't

around and Sawyer paused in his work more often than usual to engage her in conversation. To tease. Flirt. Did he think about the night they'd kissed as often as she did? He said he didn't regret it and hoped she didn't either, but had it meant anything to him at all in regards to the future? Or was it all in good fun? A pleasant distraction?

Most days having him hang around would be a special treat, one that would send her spirits soaring. But on the heels of Therese's words of caution, she couldn't respond in kind to his playful overtures without a melancholy tug to her heart.

Worst of all, though, was that the arrival of Therese and Ray's sons left her in a guilty quandary. Would Sawyer consider a potential move to California a disclosable event? Therese insisted it wouldn't happen. But could a houseful of persuasive offspring wear down their resolve?

"You're quiet today." Sawyer leaned against the door frame of the storeroom, where she was unpacking and recording incoming orders. "Are the boys doing okay?"

"Great. With the date set for the camping trip, that's all they can talk about." What had their California aunts and uncles thought of *Sawyer this* and *Sawyer that* as they all sat around the lunch table?

"Good. That should keep their minds off moving in with me." He winked. "With us."

She glanced away, knowing her cheeks were probably as pink as the plastic water bottle sitting on the floor beside her. Sawyer seemed to get a kick out of referring to them in a roundabout way as a couple, but they'd never even gone out on a date, unless you counted the fishing trip. Wouldn't a man who had *serious* intentions about a woman initiate something more substantial than kisses?

But no, they'd skipped the dating preliminaries and gone straight to the kissing. Which seemed perfectly normal at the time, considering what they'd been through together with Cubby that day. Given Therese's concerns, however, might it not be a good idea to take a step back?

"I noticed in church on Sunday," Sawyer ventured, his expression suddenly more serious, "that Therese didn't seem quite her energetic self. Is she doing okay?"

Tori froze at his abrupt change in subject, or so it seemed to Sawyer. But maybe it was his imagination? Then she shrugged and ripped open another box. "I don't think she's been sleeping that well lately."

"But otherwise she and Ray are doing okay?"

With the boys making such a point about moving in with him—and Tori—he couldn't help but wonder what had initiated that thinking. The kiss, sure. But were his earlier seemingly misguided concerns about the boys' living situation truly unfounded? Were Ray and Therese up to caring for the active youngsters? And if they weren't, what was he going to do about it? Persuade Tori to work for them full-time? See about getting additional help?

As if sensing his concerns, Tori leveled a look at him. "Don't go there, Sawyer."

"Why not? Don't you wonder why the kids suddenly fixated on moving in with me?"

"They're kids."

"Yeah, but—"

"They're living in a happy and secure home with grandparents who love them." She paused before ripping open another box. "But you're not alone in your concerns. Therese is concerned, as well."

"She is?"

"Of course." Tori gave him a "get a clue" look. "She was caught off guard when they announced their intentions to move to your place. But like I told her, kids are kids. They're attracted to whatever seems the most fun and new at the moment."

"Right now I'm the flavor of the month?"

"You are." She stood and stretched her cramped legs. "Which is something you may want to give some serious thought to as you become reacquainted with your brothers."

"How do you mean?"

"Well…" Why'd she look as if pursuing this thread of conversation might not be a good idea after all? "How involved do you consider you were with the kids before their parents died?"

He shifted his shoulder where he'd propped it against the door frame. "Pretty involved, I guess."

"So you were around from the time they were little?"

"Quite a bit."

"I imagine the boys got attached to you."

"Where are you going with this, Tori?"

Again she paused as she moved to lean against the door frame opposite him, and he got a bad feeling that maybe he didn't want to hear what she was about to say.

"If you're still wondering what that 'something' is that stands between you and the Selbys…well, this is it."

"What's 'it'?"

"They feel," she said quietly, "that you abandoned the boys after your dad died. Left them without a familiar, much-loved face, a solid foundation in a world that had turned upside down."

He shook his head in denial. "Therese and Ray were their solid base. Not me."

"Like you told me and Therese confirmed, they weren't around that much when the boys were very small. So the twins weren't as close to them as they were to you at the time of their parents' death."

"They're blaming me because I didn't maintain a close relationship with my little brothers, is that it? They have a selective memory is all I can say. After they took the boys in, I got the impression they didn't want me hanging around."

"They're not blaming. They have nothing but good things to say about you."

Yeah, right. "There's got to be a big *except* in there someplace."

"Except—" she acknowledged, meeting his gaze evenly, "that they feel you let your brothers down. Twice. And now they're concerned that with the boys again gravitating toward you, you'll disappear."

"No way." Especially not after God safely returned Cubby to them and that close call hammered home just how important those little guys were to him. They were blood of his blood. *Family.* "I'm in it for the long haul."

Couldn't Tori see how important his brothers were to him? Understand how hard it had been to get involved again even at her urging, knowing that Ray and Therese had reasons to disapprove of him whether they realized it or not? And yet, now Tori was saying they *didn't* disapprove of him—except for thinking he'd deserted the boys?

Oh, man.

Ray and Therese's excessive caution, their sometimes less-than-welcoming behavior…as much as he hated to acknowledge it, it made sense now.

"I'm sorry, Sawyer, but I thought you needed to know."

"I had no idea they thought anything like that. No idea that I hurt the twins." His heart aching, he met Tori's steady gaze. "I didn't mean to."

Her smile wobbled as she stepped forward to wrap

her arms around him, rested the side of her face on his chest. "I know you didn't."

He'd had the best of intentions when pulling away from the boys. But because he didn't understand the full picture, his best intentions—and his persistent guilt—backfired on him.

He slipped his arms around Tori, laying his head against hers. "Thank you for telling me, Tori."

But how was he going to rectify this one?

And what must Tori think of him now? Even if he were ready to broach the subject of a courtship, on top of this misunderstanding with the Selbys that would be a surefire way to get shown the door.

They stood together for some time, neither saying a word. Tori knew this revelation wounded Sawyer. She could see it in his eyes. Hear it in his voice.

Had she betrayed Therese by divulging to him their private conversation? But how could she let him continue to wonder what stood between him and a stronger relationship with his brothers' grandparents? How terribly sad that this misunderstanding between grieving people had gone on for so long, wounded so deeply. Impacted the twins.

"I think—" Sawyer's words came as a whisper "—that recruiting you to watch over the Cubster and Landon is the smartest decision I've ever made in my life. What I didn't anticipate, though, is that you'd be watching over me, too."

She smiled as his arms tightened around her. What she wouldn't give to stay here, cradled close to him for the rest of her life. One day he was Sawyer Banks, a potential employer she suspected of ulterior motives regarding the role he intended her to play in the lives of the twins.

And now? Now he was a man she'd so greatly come to care for in such a short time. To admire. To love?

Now he was *her* Sawyer.

"Penny for your thoughts," he murmured.

She couldn't share them. Not yet. They were too precious. Too fragile to voice. After Grandma passed away, her vulnerable heart had too quickly been drawn to Heath. But while at the time she thought she'd found genuine love with him, she realized now it was only a faint shadow of what was yet to come—with Sawyer. That is, if Sawyer felt the same way about her as she was coming to feel about him. If Therese's misgivings proved wrong.

He tilted her head with a gentle finger to look up at him. "My little brothers think the world of you."

"I don't know when my heart has ever been won over to children so quickly. They're so sweet. So loving."

"A lot like you in that respect." He smiled, his expression tender. And something more…

Sensing his intentions, her heartbeat quickened in anticipation. But she couldn't let him kiss her, could she? Not again. Not until they'd spent more time together. Until she discovered if Therese was wrong in her assumptions about his long-term level of devotion to the twins. To *her*.

As she well knew, the enticing feelings of "love" held little meaning if not built on a solid foundation of lasting commitment. But Sawyer had yet to speak of love. Shouldn't that fact alone put her on her guard? Enable her to resist the temptation of his kisses?

Reluctantly she pressed her hand firmly to his chest and attempted to step back.

But he held her fast, his gaze intent. "Tori, I think you need to know that—"

With a reverberating clang the cowbell above the main door startled them apart.

"Anybody home?" Diego bellowed from the front of the store.

Sawyer looked down at her almost helplessly as the sound of Diego's booted feet on the hardwood floor signaled his approach.

Rounding a display of backpacks, the young man halted abruptly, obviously taken aback at their presence and no doubt wondering why they hadn't called out in response to his greeting. He nodded to the unwieldy box in his arms. "FedEx delivered this just as I walked up."

Sawyer motioned him forward. "Put 'er in there. We were just…unpacking boxes."

"Then here's one more." Diego swiftly deposited his load, then with an uncertain glance at Tori, hurried off.

"You were starting to say?" Tori encouraged, her voice low, yet knowing that the tension-charged atmosphere that had held her breathless in Sawyer's arms was not to be recaptured.

He shrugged, avoiding her gaze. "Maybe it will come to me later."

"I guess, then, it's time I get back to the house to help with dinner." Sawyer merely nodded. And although grateful as she headed to her car that she hadn't had to disclose the Selby children's visit until she had more concrete information, the afternoon had nevertheless ended on a disquieting note.

What was it Sawyer thought she needed to know?

Chapter Seventeen

"First of all, Tori, rest assured Therese is going to be fine."

Those words met her when she stepped in the front door of the Selbys' house late that afternoon, her heart still troubled by Sawyer's unspoken words.

She stared up at the Selbys' oldest son. "What happened to her?"

"She fell down the stairs after lunch."

"Oh, no."

"We called the paramedics to check her out, but they didn't think she needed further medical attention. She's going to bruise and feel sore, though. We're to keep an eye on her, but she's upstairs resting now."

"Where are the boys?"

Curtis smiled. "Ray and Fay—sounds cute, doesn't it?—are out back playing with them so they won't disturb their grandmother."

"I'm sorry I wasn't here."

"You couldn't have done anything to prevent what happened. But I think this is a prime example of why we're getting them out of this big old house. It's too much for them, even with a housekeeper and someone to watch the twins."

"I know they've talked of getting a smaller place. Something on one level."

"That sounds like a simple enough solution," another voice called from the parlor adjacent to the entryway. Robert, son number two. Tori and Curtis entered the room to join him and his wife, Tonya, and he continued. "But they can't keep living independently. With the MS complication and two rambunctious boys, it's too much."

"Not that you're not doing a wonderful job, Tori," Tonya quickly added, her smile reassuring. "But with Ray and Therese closer to us, we can take over that responsibility."

"Although—" Robert, casting a meaningful look at his wife, sounded regretful "—it might mean splitting up the twins to manage that."

Split them up? They were talking, too, as though the decision to move Ray and Therese had been made. Had the twins' grandparents so quickly capitulated in the few hours she'd been working at the Outpost? She glanced toward the staircase that had sealed Ray and Therese's fate in the eyes of their children. "Is it okay if I go up and check on her?"

"She'll appreciate the company."

"Nice girl." Curt's voice carried up the stairs after her.

Ray and Therese's kids seemed nice enough, too, although clearly stressed by their parents' situation and the added complications presented by the children of their deceased sister. But surely they weren't serious about raising the boys in two different households?

"Tori?" a weary voice responded when she knocked at the partially open door and called Therese's name. "Please come in. And shut the door behind you."

Tori followed her employer's instructions, scanning the dimly lit room with a single lamp glowing on the nightstand next to where Therese sat upright on the bed, propped on pillows. For the first time since Tori had known her, she looked every one of her seventy-five years.

"Pull up that chair, sweetheart."

She obeyed, bringing an antique desk chair forward, and sat down. "I heard you took a bad tumble. How are you feeling?"

"Not as bad as they're making it sound. I didn't fall all the way down. I misplaced my foot not that far from the bottom. I could have done the same thing at twenty-five as at seventy-five." She motioned impatiently. "I can't believe they called 911. How embarrassing to alert the whole neighborhood to a stumble when there are no broken bones. Nothing sprained. Bruises are putting in an appearance, though."

She rolled up her sleeve, the evidence apparent.

"But what a mess this opened the door to." Therese folded her arms in a huff, then winced at the discomfort. "If our kids have anything to say about it, there will be a moving van loading us up tomorrow morning."

"Surely that's not their decision to make."

"They think I'm being stubborn, but there's no reason we can't stay right here in Hunter Ridge."

Tori gave an inward sigh of relief. "Then there's nothing to worry about, right?"

"Except I think Ray's wavering." Therese shifted against the pillows, trying to get comfortable.

"I'm sure he's concerned about you and the toll the boys may be taking on your health. He's probably looking on down the road, too."

Would the Selbys live long enough for the twins to reach adulthood? They were both so active, so youthful, it was hard to imagine that they wouldn't, but no one could predict the future.

"The boys aren't taking a toll on my health. In fact they keep me young. And I'm not ready to give up my independence." Therese scowled. "Yes, I can understand the kids wanting us to live closer to them. But with real estate prices the way they are in California, the sale of this house won't put a dent in a place of our own there. At our age we wouldn't want to start payments on a new mortgage, so we'd have no choice but to move in with one of them. That would likely mean being separated from the boys and very possibly them being separated from each other."

"I picked up on that possibility a few minutes ago, too. They seemed reluctant to do it, but it sounded as if they thought they might not have a choice."

"Tonya and Robert are empty nesters living in a two-bedroom condo—so they want Ray and me to move in with them. Amber and Paul have a high-rise apartment and one teen still living at home, but could take one twin. Then Curtis and Fay have a house full of teenagers, but they think they could swing a nephew also."

"Not an ideal situation." In fact, Tori hated the idea and knew Sawyer would, too.

"If I know Curtis, though, he'll want everything resolved and tied up in a nice neat bow before he leaves. And if Ray gives in? I'll have no choice but to go along with him." She reached for Tori's hand. "So pray, sweetheart. Pray."

Pray she would. But as much as she hated the thought of delivering the news to Sawyer, she had no choice now but to let him know what was going on in the lives of his little brothers.

"They'll split up the twins over my dead body." Sawyer sat at his desk, thunderstruck at what Tori had shared after arriving early the next morning before the Outpost opened. Not only did Therese have multiple sclerosis, but Ray and Therese were possibly moving to LA and taking the boys to live with one or the other of Vanessa's older siblings.

"I'm not under the impression splitting the boys is something they want to do. They'd prefer to avoid it. But their housing situations, unfortunately, aren't conducive to taking in two more adults and caring for twin preschoolers under a single roof."

"Those boys will not be split up." But how could he stop them? They were legally in Therese and Ray's care, and if the couple went along with their children's plans… "Surely they'll stand their ground for the boys' sake."

"That's been their intention all along, but—"

"All along? This isn't the first you're learning of this?" Surely he must have misheard.

She glanced away, almost as if reluctant to look him in the eye. "They'd earlier mentioned their kids have been at them to relocate to Los Angeles since they first retired years ago. This isn't anything new."

"You've known about that possibility and never said a word to me about it? You didn't think that was something that would negatively impact my brothers?"

"There wasn't anything to tell."

"How do you figure that?"

"Because Ray and Therese were dead set against leaving Hunter Ridge. Now with Therese revealing the MS diagnosis to the family combined with yesterday's fall, they're under more pressure from the kids. Therese is still adamant she wants to raise their grandsons here. Ray's on the fence. I don't know what they'll decide."

He ran his hand roughly through his hair. "This is great. Just great."

He didn't know much about Vanessa's brothers. But he did know that the twins' folks hadn't ranked her siblings at the top of the list of potential guardians should anything happen to them before the boys reached adulthood. In fact, they'd felt strongly enough about that issue that they'd listed *him*, of all people, second after Therese and Ray. His dad wouldn't want his sons growing up in Los Angeles either. And certainly not apart. Not going through another upheaval on the heels of losing their parents.

"This is exactly what I needed to be kept in the loop on, Tori. It's why I recruited you for the job in the first place." He caught the wince in her eyes at his accusatory tone, but continued on. "This doesn't give me much time to figure out what can be done."

"You'll try to stop them from moving?"

"Ray and Therese can move to Timbuktu if they want to. But I'm not going to let them drag my brothers far from the place Dad wanted them to call home. I can't tell you how often he said he wished he could have grown up here rather than in a big city. How he said he loved the town and was thrilled his second family would get the opportunity his first one didn't."

"But would relocating with their grandparents be so bad? Ray and Therese would be nearby even if the kids weren't under the same roof. Their children seem nice. Very sincere in their concern for their parents and the boys."

"Splitting siblings up is bad enough, but twins? No." He shook his head. "I won't let that happen, and I'll use the fact that I'm legally next in line for guardianship to press my point."

"What are you going to do?"

"See a lawyer. Try to get those kids removed from

their grandparents' guardianship if I can. The boys shouldn't be held captive in Ray and Therese's power struggle with their adult children. But I'm going to need your help in this, Tori. Your support."

"How? I'm not sure—"

"You can vouch for me. A character witness. You've lived for months under the Selbys' roof and can speak to Therese's health situation and how that could impact Cubby and Landon. To how Ray forbids me to talk to the twins about our father. How healthy is that? You can advise not splitting up the twins."

"It would break Ray and Therese's hearts to give them up, even to you. And I'd have to testify in court against them? I don't want to do that."

"Tori, I'm counting on you. I owe these boys and their parents more than you can imagine."

"You don't *owe* them anything, Sawyer. Their grandparents are their legal guardians and you're the big brother. LA's—what? Ten hours away? You could go over on a long weekend every few months to see them."

He shook his head. "I owe them more than that."

"You keep saying you owe them. You owe them. Maybe if I understood—"

"If it weren't for me, Tori," he stated matter-of-factly, cutting her off, "their mom and dad would still be alive."

The confusion on her face left him instantly regretting his blunt words. But it was too late now to take them back. She was the woman he loved, though. Who better to confide in?

"I don't understand."

He stood, then moved restlessly around the confines of his office. He'd never talked about this to anyone. Had never voiced it, and he wasn't sure he could now.

"Sawyer?"

He took a steadying breath. May as well get it over with. "Dad had been out of town on Outpost business that week. When I stopped in around noon to play with the boys and drop off groceries—Vanessa was laid up with a broken leg—she mentioned that the hot water heater didn't seem to be working right. I didn't know anything about hot water heaters, so I told her I'd get hold of some-one and have them take a look at it."

"And then?" Tori's soft words prompted.

"When I left there, I got caught up in a series of Out-post emergencies and…forgot." He closed his eyes, the events unfolding before him as though it were only yes-terday. "Late that night, the water heater exploded."

He heard Tori's quick intake of breath.

"The house caught on fire. Dad drove up shortly there-after—probably hoping to surprise Vanessa by returning a day earlier than planned—and called the fire depart-ment. But before the volunteers got there, he went in himself and managed to get the boys out."

Tori stared at him, the horrors of that night no doubt playing out in her imagination.

"He put them in his truck where he'd parked away from the house and called me to come get them. Then he went back in after Vanessa before I got there. They were…both were overcome with smoke. Couldn't be re-vived."

He drew a ragged breath.

"Oh, Sawyer…"

As on the previous day, she came to him and put her arms around him. But he could only stand rigidly, over-whelmed by the memories of billowing smoke and flames leaping into the night as he sat in the truck surrounded by the ear-piercing wails of the frightened boys.

"I'm sorry." She rested her head on his chest.

"You can see, can't you, Tori, why I can't let Ray and Therese take them away? I'll do anything. I don't care what it takes. I don't care what it costs. If I lose the cabin and the Outpost, it doesn't matter."

"I understand. I do." She pulled slightly back to look up at him. "But do you think you're prepared to take on two preschoolers? You yourself assured me not long ago that's nothing you wanted any part of."

"My dad was a hero going back in there after his kids and Vanessa. The least I can do is to look out for the sons he risked his life to save."

No, he wasn't a hero like his dad. But he hadn't known the Selbys interpreted his actions after the fire as unreliable, irresponsible, uncaring.

How would *that* look in court?

With Tori's encouragement, though, he'd started anew, hadn't he? Now he had every intention of hanging in there regardless of how his heart ached over the role he'd played in their parents' deaths. The Selbys, however, weren't likely to forget his track record.

"It wasn't your fault, Sawyer, so the most important thing—" Tori drew his wandering attention "—is to forgive yourself."

He scoffed. "Like that will ever happen."

"How can God bless your future if you don't let go of the past? If your dad and his wife could be here right now, that's what they'd tell you to do. I know they would. They wouldn't want you crippled for life over something that you didn't do intentionally, that probably couldn't have been averted even if you'd immediately called a repairman. What are the odds one would have foreseen the potential for such a tragedy and dropped everything to get there that afternoon?"

"What if one had?"

"The likelihood of that is slim. You've got to let it go, Sawyer."

"No chance of that unless I can prevent the boys from being taken away. Will you help me, Tori? My mind is racing to what it may take to gain legal guardianship of my brothers. The Selbys will fight me on this and I can't blame them."

"Maybe they won't. Maybe you can talk to them… ask their forgiveness for what they mistakenly perceive as you abandoning your brothers. There's no need to tell them about the false guilt that drove you away."

"Then how would they understand?" He stepped back from her. "Besides, I've done nothing with my life to lead them to believe I'd be a good long-term influence on the boys. I'm not an established family man. I'm soon to be thirty and still unmarried. No church involvement after Dad died. Basically I snubbed my nose at God for way too long."

"But you no longer do."

"I've run into financial problems this past year, too," he continued, barely hearing her. "And while I haven't advertised that any more than I did my gambling past, this is a small town, so there's probably not much of anything that is secret. The Selbys would laugh right in my face."

If only there was a way to show his little brothers' grandparents that he'd be a good role model. That he'd bring the twins up to honor God, respect others, be good citizens. If only…

And then, as he stared in anguish at Tori, it hit him.

Hadn't his mind been filled with the possibility yesterday when he'd held Tori so tenderly in his arms? When he'd lain awake in the night imagining what a lifetime with her would be like? Wondering how soon he could afford a ring?

He'd long heard talk of how God worked behind the scenes to put people in the right place at the right time. Bible stories he'd grown up on emphasized that over and over. Would Tori see the amazing grace of the timing of their relationship, too? His spirits lifting, he again moved in closer and reached for her hand, thankfulness over-flowing his heart that she was in his life at this time of crisis.

God *did* answer prayers.

"Alone, I'm sunk, Tori. But together, we might stand a chance." He tilted his head, his eyes searching hers. "So what do you think? Would you be willing to partner with me to make this happen?"

"What are you talking about, Sawyer?"

"Us. A couple. Mr. and Mrs."

Her eyes widened.

Impulsively dropping to one knee, he was flooded with joy as he smiled confidently up at her. "Will you do me the honor of marrying me, Miss Janner?"

Chapter Eighteen

Tori's breath caught as she gazed down at him.

How many times in the past few weeks had she, like a starry-eyed adolescent, daydreamed about this very moment? About where they'd be. What he'd say. How she'd respond.

Too often her imagination had leaped ahead to visions of sewing her wedding dress. Decorating *their* cabin. Planning a life together. But she'd reined in those racing thoughts as premature. It hadn't been long ago that another man told her he loved her. Had given her a ring.

No, this time, she'd decided after Therese expressed concerns, she'd take it slow. She and Sawyer would build on the foundation it appeared God might be laying and, who knew, maybe by year's end they'd be engaged.

But Sawyer wasn't taking his time. In fact, he was off and running. Why?

She laughed uneasily. "I'm afraid you've left me speechless."

He grinned. "Only takes one word."

One word. She was one word away from walking down the aisle on the arm of the man she loved. *Mrs. Sawyer Banks.*

An unexpected knot tightened in her chest. What if…? She pressed her hand to her mouth, tears pricking her eyes.

Sawyer sobered. "What's wrong?"

Barely able to breathe, her words came out a broken whisper. "Why are you doing this, Sawyer?"

"Why?" He laughed. "Because I want to marry you."

"When?"

Puzzlement momentarily lit his eyes. "As soon as we can, I guess."

This sickish feeling in the pit of her stomach was nothing like her dreams of a proposal. *Please, God, I don't want to mess this up. But I have to be sure.*

She wet her lips. Forced herself to speak in a normal, if somewhat shaky voice. "Do you want to marry me because as your wife I'll lend you that coveted family-man status? Because being married might convince the Selbys that the boys will be in good hands with the two of us in parental roles rather than you alone? Because you think that if you have me by your side they won't be so inclined to fight you in court?"

His smile faded as he slowly rose to his feet.

"That's not where I'm coming from. Sure, Therese and Ray think the world of you. So do the boys. They might be willing to see the advantages of us—together—taking the boys in. But—"

"You're saying you're *not* scrambling to find a way to keep the boys from going to LA?"

"Don't you trust me?" he said softly as a muscle in his jaw tightened. "Surely you believe Cubby and Landon would be happiest in my—our—care?"

A sense of foreboding washed over her at his expressionless tone. At the hurt so clearly evident in his eyes.

"It's just that this is so sudden. And the timing—"

He stared at her as if not believing what he was hearing. "You think they'd be better off living in a big city with aunts and uncles they don't know rather than living with me?"

"Don't put words in my mouth." Her tone was sharper than intended. She was shaking now, deep down inside. *God, how can I be sure?*

Despite his denials, how could she be certain this sudden rush to matrimony had nothing to do with bolstering his image with the Selbys and in court? That he hadn't, as she'd originally suspected months ago, planned all along for her to aid him in taking the boys from their grandparents?

Please, God, I love him. But I can't marry a man who isn't marrying me for the right reasons, can I? A man who hasn't so much as uttered a single word about loving me.

Trembling, she moved to the office door, her back to him. She had to get out of here. Far from the wounded look in Sawyer's beautiful blue eyes. "I can't marry you, Sawyer. Not under the current circumstances."

Maybe not under *any* circumstances.

"Tori, wait. Can't we—"

"No," she said as she jerked the door open. Not daring to look at him, knowing how she was letting him down, she fled the room.

He didn't follow.

He'd jumped the gun and blown it.

Convinced God had amazingly brought her into his life when he needed her support most, he'd thought she'd recognize it, too. She cared for him. He *knew* she did, just as he cared for her. He'd thought she'd be excited to see, with God's involvement, that there was no such thing as a coincidence. That theirs was a love match He'd ideally timed. That she'd be on the same page with him. But how could she be?

He stared glumly into his bathroom mirror early that evening as, the electric razor buzzing annoyingly, he shaved away his five-o'clock shadow to make himself presentable to meet with Therese and Ray. Stupidly, he hadn't given it a single thought that Tori hadn't been privy to his inner musings in recent days. His prayers. She hadn't listened in on his contemplations through the night when he'd wished his folks could meet her. When he pondered the timing of confessing his feelings and popping the question. Speculated on how long she'd make him wait before they tied the knot.

How could he have so majorly bungled everything? With Tori having shared with him the situation in the Selby household, comforting him after his confession about the fire and listening to his rant about being willing to do *anything* to keep his brothers in Hunter Ridge, was it any wonder she'd taken his out-of-the-blue proposal the wrong way?

How could he have left out the most important part of it?

That he *loved* her?

He'd even been about to tell her that yesterday when Diego interrupted, then had gotten cold feet. But today? He'd never been especially good at expressing his emotions. But he'd been thinking it. Feeling it. Why hadn't his mouth *said* it?

"Yeah, Louie," he said, glancing at the dog patiently watching in the bathroom's open doorway, "your human is an idiot."

The pooch thumped his tail in sympathy.

Now he'd hurt Tori. Given her the impression he wasn't serious about marrying her for love. Right from the get-go when he'd interviewed her, she'd been suspicious of his motives for wanting her to apply for the position. Now, as far as she was concerned, the pieces to the puzzle were fitting together.

Except that wasn't the way it was at all.

With a groan that startled Louie, he headed downstairs and passed by the kitchen, where Blackie joined them. Was it only this morning that he was scrambling eggs and thinking about what it might be like to prepare breakfast for *her*? To serve it on a tray with a fresh rose from the garden when she awakened? To shower her with kisses?

Now, though, she wasn't even speaking to him. He'd tried to call her several times, but his calls went straight to voice mail. And to add to his anguish, he had no idea what had been going on at the Selbys' today. Had they already drawn straws to see who took which twin?

For a fleeting moment this morning when Tori had stormed from his office, he'd been tempted to lash out in anger at God for getting his hopes up that he'd finally found someone to love—who loved him back—only to have those hopes dashed again. But it was his own fault. Not God's. And right now he needed the God of the universe on his side to keep Ray and Therese from taking Landon and Cubby to California. *To win Tori back.*

He stepped out onto the front porch and lifted his gaze skyward. "Lord, I'm undeserving. I know You won't argue with that. But I'm choosing faith in You this time. Choosing to give You a chance to work this all out. To heal the mess I've made of everything."

The first step, though, in hopes of avoiding all but minimal involvement with the court system, was meeting with the Selbys. He'd called ahead. They were expecting him, no doubt curious as to what he wanted to see them about. And once they gave him an answer—either way—God willing, he'd make things right with Tori.

Still shaken from that morning's aborted proposal, it had been all Tori could do to stay focused on caring for the boys throughout the day. Sawyer had called several times, but didn't leave a message. She'd have to talk to him eventually. She hadn't intended to hurt him by her refusal to be a part of his plan to keep the boys, but she knew she had. Deeply. She needed time to think, though. To pray. Unfortunately, she got precious little of either once she arrived back at the house.

The twins seemed abnormally anxious and whiny, which wasn't surprising considering six strangers had been in the house for a couple of days. Routines had been upset. For the first time in quite a while, she'd caught Landon blatantly lying about something, and Cubby had gotten teary over the silliest of things. But children were sensitive, and they'd undoubtedly picked up on the undercurrent of tension among the adults.

After cleaning up from the evening meal, she went upstairs to check on the twins, arriving just short of the open doorway to the bedroom when she heard a feminine voice. One of the daughters-in-law, no doubt, making an effort to get to know Cubby and Landon. Tori started to turn away, not wanting to interrupt, when she caught the unexpected words.

"Which one of you wants to come live with me?"

Shocked, knowing that all had agreed not to say anything to the boys about their possible relocation, she moved to the open door.

Over by the window Paul's wife, Amber, hands on her ample hips, smiled down at the boys. She was a fun, merry sort who probably had most kids eating out of her hand.

Landon's face took on the dark dimensions of a thundercloud. "I don't want to live with you."

Cubby shook his head. "Me neither."

Amber leaned over and put her arm around Cubby. Pulled him in close. "There's a swimming pool. I hear you like to swim."

Cubby jerked away. "I don't like your swimming pool."

"You haven't even seen it." Amber sounded somewhat irritated and, catching a glimpse of Tori in the doorway, gave her a laughingly exasperated "oh, brother" look.

Cubby's lower lip protruded. "I want to live with G'ma and G'pa."

Just then Landon spied Tori and moved in close to take her hand. "Or with Tori and Sawyer."

"Yeah." Cubby hurried over as well, and grasped her other hand. "Tori and Sawyer."

For a moment Amber looked mystified.

"Who's—oh, yeah, right. He's your big brother." She eyed Tori curiously. "So you and their—"

"No." She looked down at the boys, who were gazing up at her. She didn't want to talk about Sawyer in front of them. She slipped her hands from theirs and patted them on their backs. "Why don't you two put your toys away while your aunt Amber and I visit a bit? Then I'll be back to help you get cleaned up for bedtime."

Reluctantly, but remembering their grandpa's rules about dragging their feet at bedtime, they scurried off to pick up the toys littering the floor, effectively ignoring their aunt.

Amber joined her, and Tori pulled the door shut, then they moved farther down the hallway.

"Cute kids. But it's kind of like trying to pick out a puppy, isn't it?"

Tori knew she was attempting to be funny, but somehow she couldn't join in this aunt's amusement. The boys weren't puppies and she hated the idea of them being separated.

"I'm sure you've gotten attached to them," Amber ventured again as they continued down the hall. "Clearly they're attached to you. You're going to be a hard act to follow."

"They're very loving. It just takes a while for them to warm up to new people." Tori offered a conciliatory smile. "They're tired tonight, too."

"I think they'd like the pool."

"I'm sure they would." Tori drew to a halt. "I know you meant well, trying to get to know them, but everyone agreed not to talk to the boys about a possible move for fear of upsetting them. There's been no final decision on relocation one way or another."

Amber sighed. "You know, though, what it's going to come down to. Either now or in the very near future. I mean this MS thing…"

"I know you're all doing what you can to deal with a difficult situation." Tori had done her best to stay out of the family dispute, but maybe Amber needed to be enlightened. "You may not be aware, though, that MS isn't one-size-fits-all. The progression of it varies from person to person. Therese may not have any further deterioration. She's done very well for quite some time. It's my understanding they're making great strides in medications."

"But we can't risk it, can we? That something like the fall would happen again and no one would be here."

"Anyone can fall."

"Amber?" Paul peered into the hallway from the guest

room, raising a cell phone in his hand. "Our eldest wants to talk to you."

When Amber hurried off, Tori's heart ached for all involved. But it troubled her that if it turned out the boys and their grandparents had to move to California, she couldn't deny the role she'd played in the outcome. Did Sawyer feel she'd betrayed him by not speaking up earlier? By not standing at his side now?

Although she'd been careful not to divulge confidences shared with her by Therese and Ray, *had* she waited too long? Put Sawyer in a position where there wasn't time to take legal action should it be necessary? Left him between a rock and a hard place where his sole option was to marry the very woman who'd let him down?

Would marrying her lend him credibility in the eyes of the Selbys? A judge?

She loved him. Loved the boys. But was that a strong enough basis for marrying a man who wanted her to be his wife for all the wrong reasons, no matter how well-intentioned? Would God bless such a marriage? Or did He, in His great wisdom, already have good plans for the future of the twins in a new home with their mother's family?

Regardless, though, she needed to let Ray and Therese know that despite her promise, Amber had been talking to the twins about a possible move.

Heading down the stairs, she glimpsed Ray quietly motioning Therese into the library, then closing the double doors. Disappointed that she'd missed them, but unwilling to interrupt, Tori had just made it to the bottom of the stairs when the doorbell chimed. With a sigh, she moved to open it.

Sawyer. As handsome and determined-looking as ever.

Was he here to argue his case again? To try to change her mind?

"Sawyer, I—"

"I'm here to see Ray and Therese." His words were low. Clipped and impersonal. "They're expecting me."

He wasn't here to see her. He'd decided to appeal to the boys' grandparents on his own. Did he stand a chance as a single man who'd long had a rocky relationship with his brothers' grandparents? Or was it a lost cause?

She stepped back. "They're in the library."

He nodded and moved down the hall to the door off the entryway.

Starting up the staircase again to see to the boys, she couldn't help pausing to look down at him. Still standing outside the library doors. Shoulders squared. Head down.

In prayer?

Admiration swelled within her. He was a brave man. A good man. A man who'd grown up without his mom and carried a heavy burden for the loss of his father. Seeing him standing there, alone, ready to step out in faith although the likelihood of success was slim, touched a place deep within her heart.

I love him, Father God. And I love his little brothers. As she stood gazing down at the man silently waiting outside the door, an unexpected peace settled into her heart. A startling sense of direction. Assurance. She loved Sawyer. She'd make him a good wife. A good mother to Cubby and Landon.

And one day, might he come to love her as much as she loved him, regardless of his motivation for wanting to marry her?

She swallowed, curiously aware of the beat of her own heart—and the presence of the man she loved. Quietly she descended the steps and approached him, his head still bowed. She reached for his hand.

Startled, he looked up, his gaze searching hers.

"In answer to this morning's question, Sawyer—" She offered a smile, praying she was making the right decision. "I love you. And yes, I will marry you."

Chapter Nineteen

Hope exploding, he stared at her. "Are you sure? I don't want—"

"One hundred percent."

But even with Tori—his now-fiancée—at his side, it was still a long shot. She'd said she loved him. Her actions declared she trusted him. That she'd willingly marry him in spite of his faults and shortcomings and blundering ways. That's how God accepted His children, not because they were perfect—in fact, far from it—but because He loved them.

"Thank you, Tori." *And thank You, God.* He leaned in to kiss her on the cheek, then took a steadying breath and knocked at the door.

When they entered the library hand in hand, Ray and Therese exchanged a look he wasn't sure how to interpret. Surprise, maybe, but something else, as well.

"Please sit down." Ray motioned to the sofa across from where Therese was seated, but he remained standing by the fireplace.

Sawyer and Tori sat down and although an army of butterflies hammered his insides, he gathered courage from the warmth of her hand in his. Courage from the knowledge that no matter what happened in the coming minutes, Tori would be by his side for a lifetime.

He cleared his throat. "We—Tori and I—are here to make a request regarding the future of my brothers."

Ray raised a brow. "Both of you?"

Sawyer's eyes smiled briefly into Tori's, then he gave Ray a confident nod. "We're engaged to be married."

Therese gasped. "I was afraid that— Ray and I both thought— I mean, we—" She stopped, looking embarrassed.

"What she means—" Ray smiled at his wife "—is we've suspected there was something special growing between you two, but—"

Sawyer gave them both a reassuring look. "But you love Tori and thought I wouldn't make a commitment."

Nodding, Therese exchanged a look with her husband. Undoubtedly they'd been afraid that, as with his brothers, he'd get close to Tori and walk away. Break her heart.

"I offer my congratulations." Ray stepped forward to kiss Tori on the cheek, then he pinned a sharp gaze on Sawyer as he turned to shake hands. "In a very short time, we've come to love Tori like another daughter. So remember, we're the equivalent of in-laws you'll have to deal with if you—"

"Don't worry, Ray. I'm in it for the long haul."

"You better be." But the older man's eyes were smiling as he again moved back to the fireplace. "So you're here to talk about the twins?"

Sawyer glanced at Tori and she nodded. "Tori's shared with me that you may be moving to California and taking the boys with you."

"That's not yet been decided," Therese hurried to make clear. It sounded as if she wasn't yet ready to throw in the towel to the demands of her offspring.

Ray gave her a fleeting frown. "But it's likely."

Tori squeezed Sawyer's hand, her encouraging gaze urging him on.

"With that possibility in mind, we'd like to make a proposal and ask that you give it serious consideration."

"Go on."

"Dad was big on wanting Cubby and Landon to grow up in a small town. He wished he could have grown up outside of a big metropolitan area himself. Wished that he and my mother could have raised my other two brothers and me in a place like Hunter Ridge." He looked from Ray to Therese, praying their hearts would be open to what he had to say. "I—Tori and I—would like, with your blessing, to open our home to my little brothers and raise them in Hunter Ridge. Like Vanessa and Dad wanted."

Tears pricked Therese's eyes as her gaze sought that of her husband.

"We don't expect an immediate answer," Tori quickly inserted. "Please take your time to think about it. Pray about it. We know how much you love the twins. How much you want the best for them."

"We love them, too," Sawyer added, "and promise to take good care of them. Be there for them. To raise them in a godly home."

He waited with bated breath as, for what seemed an eternity, neither responded. Too shocked at the out-of-the-blue request, or adamantly against it and wanting to word a rejection diplomatically?

"Ray?" Therese whispered, her eyes questioning.

"What Therese would like me to share with you is that, as Tori's aware, having the boys in our lives this past year has been both a challenge and a blessing."

Therese nodded.

"Admittedly there have been adjustments, having been

retired for a good ten years and empty nesters for longer than that. We've made mistakes." He leveled a look at Sawyer. "Both in our dealings with the boys—and with you."

"We've come to recognize, Sawyer," Therese said, "that the loss of your father hit you hard. That you were witness to the tragic events that night. That the sense of helplessness and anger must still be overpowering. How difficult it must be to be around the boys at times, a reminder of that day and your shared loss. Ray and I—we apologize for not understanding. For not being a better support to you. We were caught up—so overwhelmed with our own loss—with the arrival of the boys—that—"

"There's no need to apologize, Therese." Sawyer didn't want them bearing a burden of guilt such as the one he'd too long carried. "I take responsibility for not being there for *you* when you took the boys in. I could have made the adjustment easier for you. But I dropped the ball."

Ray leveled a reassuring look at him. "I think we've *all* dropped our fair share of balls in the past year or so, Sawyer. We all had needs and expectations of each other that none of us adequately communicated. But the boys needed us, and Vanessa and Anderson made us their legal guardians should anything happen to them. None of us, of course, ever thinking at the time we agreed to it that the responsibility printed on paper would too soon become a reality."

"Ray and I've come to realize that despite best intentions, at this time in our lives we're better at grandparenting than we are parenting." Therese clasped her hands tightly. "And with the size of this house becoming a millstone around our necks and the uncertainties of the MS..."

Ray cleared his throat. "After that diagnosis a number

of years ago, we'd intended to downsize here in Hunter Ridge. But with the boys joining us, well, that didn't seem like an option. And our kids are right. That's not a long-term solution for the boys."

Tori again squeezed Sawyer's hand. He knew she was praying as hard as he was.

"Which is why I'm—if not yet Therese—giving serious consideration to a California move. As much as we love Hunter Ridge and could probably continue for some time to make it on our own here as a couple, we have the boys' welfare to consider, too."

Please, God, give me the strength to accept whatever decision Ray is leading up to. It's not looking good. But I don't know if I have the heart to take them to court. To try to wrestle my little brothers away from them.

Tori's hand tightened once more on his.

"Our children are willing to take us in," Ray continued, his expression solemn. "To take the boys, too. They've been good parents to their own children. Raised them in happy, supportive homes. That considered…"

Please, God.

"That considered," Ray reiterated, "we'd still prefer to raise our grandsons in Hunter Ridge. Which is why—"

Tori held her breath. *Please. Please.*

"It's why we've been praying that God would help us find a way to do that," Therese concluded, her eyes bright with tears. "And it appears the two of you may be the answer to those prayers."

Sawyer glanced at Tori uncertainly. No doubt wondering, like her, if he'd heard right. "You're saying…?"

Ray stepped away from the fireplace. "We're saying that if you are willing to take the boys into your home, we'll plan to stay in Hunter Ridge."

Therese was openly crying now, and Ray moved to clasp a hand to her shoulder.

Sawyer's stunned gaze met Tori's. "We're more than willing."

Tori's mouth suddenly went dry. *They were getting married. Taking in Cubby and Landon.* A disorienting, momentary regret washed through her, but she pushed it away. She'd made a commitment to the man she loved, even if he wasn't marrying her for the same reason. As far as it depended on her, she'd make their relationship work. God would help her, wouldn't he?

Ray gave a relieved laugh. "I doubt there will be much convincing of the twins to do since you offer a country place, dogs and room for a pony."

"I honestly don't know what to say—" Sawyer smiled tentatively, still trying to take it all in "—except thank you."

Therese wiped away tears as she stood to give them both a hug. "No, thank *you* both. You're enabling us to remain in Hunter Ridge. This is our home. This is where we want to live out our remaining days. Now we can do it and still be a part of our grandsons' lives."

"You can count on it." The joy in Sawyer's voice confirmed Tori's decision. "They need their grandparents. Tori and I wouldn't have it any other way."

Everything would be okay. She had to believe that.

Ray clapped him on the back. "So, when's the wedding?"

Sawyer's face reddened. No wonder. They'd only been engaged thirty seconds before they'd walked into the library together.

"We want to talk to Pastor McCrae before we set a date," she ad-libbed, amused at the relief her response brought to Sawyer's eyes. "Sometime this summer, we expect."

"We need to pick out a ring, too," he added, sounding apologetic for that omission.

Ray laughed. "Got ahead of yourself, did you, Banks?"

"Always."

A smiling Therese took her husband's hand. "If you two will excuse us, I think Ray and I need to call a family meeting. Let the kids know there's been a change in plans."

Ray pretended to cringe. "They aren't going to like the fact that we're not moving to LA, but with the responsibility for the boys being shifted—the four of us can meet with our lawyers next week—we're in a good position to stand our ground and make a case for remaining in Hunter Ridge."

When the Selbys left the room, Sawyer closed the doors behind them, set the lock, then turned to her, uncertainty in his eyes.

"Here we are," she said brightly, unsure of what else there was to say as she attempted to push aside a persistent ache in her heart. They'd gone straight from a heated disagreement to engagement and pending guardianship of two little boys. Before they stepped in to meet with Ray and Therese, she'd told him she loved him.

He'd merely said *thank you*.

He slowly approached her. "I'm sorry, Tori."

It was a little late for apologies, wasn't it? There was no going back now. They had two little boys to think of.

"I hope you can find it in your heart to forgive me."

"Sawyer—" They had a lot to discuss. Eventually. But right now wasn't the time. She was tired. She wanted him to go home and for the day to end.

"Listen. Please? I apologize for accusing you of not

telling me about the Selbys' kids wanting them to move to California."

He wasn't apologizing for marrying her to keep the boys?

"You are a person of integrity," he continued, "and you honored the privacy of your employers. You've done everything possible not to compromise that yet keep the best interests of the boys in mind. It was a no-win situation. And I was wrong. Forgive me?"

How could she not? She nodded, then drew a shaky breath "Now what?"

He ducked his head and looked up at her, a playful twinkle in his eye. "Pick out a ring?"

The heaviness in her heart increased. "Sawyer, you don't have to pretend. I understand."

His forehead wrinkled. "Pretend what?"

"Pretend that this marriage is for real."

"What are you talking about?"

"I'm not backing out of this. But you don't need to pretend you're crazy in love with me just because I'm madly in love with you."

"Who's pretending?" He took her hand and tugged her closer. "Tori Janner, I am completely and utterly besotted with you."

"But I thought—"

"Don't tell me you still have it in your head that I want to marry you in hopes of gaining custody of the boys?" His forehead furrowed. "What's a man have to do to—"

Before she could stop him, he leaned in for a long, lingering kiss.

When he finally drew away, he gazed down at her knowingly. "Didn't I tell you earlier that I hoped that says it all? I love you, Tori. I'll always love you. The kind of love that leads to wedding bells and baby diapers and golden anniversaries."

He loved her. He meant it.

"I want all that, too, Sawyer." Her eyes smiled into his. "And more."

He chuckled as she pulled him closer to renew the kiss, and for the longest time ever her heart danced as she relished the tender warmth of his lips. The strength of his arms. The distinct awareness of God smiling down on them.

At the sound of children's voices in the hallway, he reluctantly drew back, his voice husky as he gazed into her eyes. "Get the picture now, Tori?"

"I—" Her words came breathlessly. "I…think so."

"Good. But if you need any more convincing, I'm more than happy to oblige."

The door knob rattled. "Tori? Are you in there? Our toys are put away now."

She smiled. "Landon."

"Can we come in?"

"And the Cubster," Sawyer echoed with a grin. "You know, don't you, that this is probably a taste of what life's going to be like from here on out?"

"We'll have to get extremely clever at grabbing stolen moments."

"And invest in good locks."

"Sawyer? Tori?" Little fists pounded the doors. "We hear you. We know you're in there."

Sawyer raised a brow. "Should we let them in?"

"I don't think we have much choice."

He pressed a kiss to her hand. "I love you."

"And I love you."

Together they walked to the double doors, where Sawyer flipped the lock and flung them wide.

Momentarily startled, the twins stared up at them. Then breaking into laughter, they launched themselves into welcoming arms.

Epilogue

"Sawyer's my big brother, but he's gonna kinda be my new dad, too." Landon, a bow tie coordinating with his dress shirt and pants, lifted his chin as if challenging his Sunday school buddies to call him a liar.

"Yeah," Cubby, similarly dressed, piped up proudly before the friends crowding around them at Pastor Mc-Crae's wedding reception could dispute his twin. "We'll have *two* dads. Kind of. One in Heaven and a pretend one down here. Right, Tori? And *you'll* be our second mom."

The twins looked to her for confirmation and Tori's heart melted at the trust in their eyes. How dearly God had blessed her in recent months, with Sawyer and his young siblings topping the list.

"Yes, I'll be your second mom. I can hardly wait." She didn't know if the boys would ever choose to call her Mom, but she was okay with it if they didn't. She didn't need to share the title with the boys' much-loved deceased parent. But it was evident that they saw her and their half brother in parental roles and accepted it. Were excited about it.

"Tori's marrying our brother," Landon clarified for

his little friends. "And then we're going to live together in Sawyer's cabin. He has *two* dogs."

The others immediately bombarded the twins with questions about their new pets, the prospect of a wedding immediately dismissed for the more important aspects of the anticipated union. Canine pals.

Smiling, she left them to their excited explanations and joined the growing circle of guests at the cake table, where Jodi and Garrett were posing for pictures. Childhood pals, now husband and wife.

A tingle of anticipation skimmed through Tori as she watched the newlyweds laugh and joke with the photographer and their friends. Two more months and she and Sawyer would be cutting their own cake. Eight weeks, which was more than enough time to finish her wedding dress and Sunshine's bridesmaid one. Plenty of time to ready the cabin for her and, eventually, the boys' arrival when the legalities were finalized. This coming week, too, she'd submit the best of her quilting samples to the Hunter Ridge Artists' Co-op for evaluation, so prayers were focused on that venture for a good outcome.

She was already planning a celebration in their new home with Therese and Ray as their honored guests. The couple hoped before summer's end to move out of their too-big house, and in the coming years, Tori would make sure the boys' grandparents were included in every family event they wanted to be.

"Hey, pretty lady," a familiar male voice whispered in her ear. A strong arm slipped around her waist and pulled her close. "Thanks for agreeing not to stuff me into one of those penguin suits."

Smiling, she turned to Sawyer, so handsome with his blond hair tumbling over his forehead. The twinkle in his eyes sent her heart twirling as she reached out to straighten his bolo tie. "I wouldn't think of it. Not your style."

His free hand captured hers, and he gave it a quick kiss.

"Hey, knock it off, you two." Ray, who'd moved in quietly next to them, nodded toward the cake table. "This show is supposed to be focused on the two up there, remember?"

"Spoilsport," Sawyer mumbled under his breath.

"You know Tori's too good for you, don't you?" Ray continued. "I hope you're getting down on your knees each night and thanking God that love is blind—to many things."

"You're not telling me anything I don't know." Sawyer's eyes smiled into hers. "You sure won't catch me taking this little lady for granted. Ever."

"Keep that promise, boy, and you'll have a long and happy marriage."

Sawyer's arm tightened around her waist. "That's the plan."

"Shhh." A woman behind Sawyer motioned them to silence. "They're about to cut the cake."

As always at this climactic moment of a wedding reception, Tori watched with bated breath as together the couple sliced the tiered white cake. A laughing Garrett grasped a thickly frosted slice and lifted it slowly to Jodi's lips. Then he drew it back again, leaving her momentarily open mouthed like a baby bird waiting to be fed. He cocked his head in question at those waiting to see what he'd do next.

He was such a tease. But please, oh, please, don't let him cram it into her mouth and smoosh it across her face as had become a practice at too many wedding receptions Tori had attended.

"Come on, buddy, let her have it," Sawyer whispered in Tori's ear, knowing how she loathed the custom.

She elbowed him, and he laughed softly.

On edge, she watched as the ever-playful Garrett leaned in to briefly touch his lips to Jodi's, then, with a melodramatic pause and a bit of eyebrow-waggling at their guests, he carefully slipped a small piece of the cake into her mouth. Kissed her again. A cheer rose from the crowded room.

"He had you going, didn't he?" Sawyer's eyes danced at her obvious relief.

"All I can say is you'd better not plan any cake-smooshing high jinks at *our* reception, buster. Not unless you plan to spend your honeymoon on the sofa by your lonely self."

His eyes widened. "You'd do that to me?"

"Your choice."

"I'd listen to her, Sawyer," Ray interrupted as Therese took her place by his side. "When Tori lays down the law to the twins, she doesn't back down. I wouldn't take any chances."

His wife looped her arm through Ray's. "Is your fiancée having to lay down the law to you, Sawyer? Already?"

"Sure sounds like it." He winked at Tori.

"We're merely establishing a few ground rules before signing on the dotted line." She teasingly gazed up at her fiancé. *Oh, how she loved him.* "Just so there won't be any surprises."

The older woman laughed. "Honey, surprises are half the fun of being married."

Sawyer nudged her. "Hear that?"

"Well, if you smoosh cake in my face on our wedding day, you may get more surprises than you're counting on."

"That's the spirit." A grinning Ray nodded approvingly. "Stand your ground. The less he gets away with at the start, the shorter his training period will be."

Therese muffled a laugh. "Like even after over fifty years of marriage I've gotten you trained? In my dreams."

"Grandma! Grandma!" Voices of two soon-to-be-kindergartners heralded the arrival of the twins.

Landon tugged on Therese's hand. "Is it time to go now? We're tired of these ties."

"You said," Cubby stated solemnly, "that we could leave after they cut the cake and go get ice cream."

"You did say that." Ray exchanged a reminding look with his wife, then turned to the twins. "So give Sawyer and Tori a hug and we'll be on our way."

He didn't have to prompt them twice, and immediately Tori had her arms filled with little boys who almost squeezed the life out of her. Then gazing into two pairs of eyes as blue as their older brother's, she brushed back their unruly blond hair.

"I love you, Tori," Cubby whispered.

Not to be outdone, Landon hugged her again. "I love you more."

Cubby frowned. "No, you don't."

"Do, too."

"Uh-uh."

"Now, boys—" Sawyer crouched next to them. "We can all love her the same, can't we? Hmm?"

After a long, glaring pause, they gave grudging nods. Then each grasping the hand of a grandparent and waving goodbye, they headed toward one of the fellowship hall's exits.

"So how about you? Are you ready to go?" Sawyer rose to his feet, a raised brow reminding her that he'd promised a long woodland walk once they'd changed from their dress clothes. "Or are you holding out for cake and punch?"

"Actually, I had my eye on those pink-and-white mints."

He cast her a sidelong glance. "The pink-and-white ones, huh?"

She nodded.

"While I don't want to deprive you, I think I can make it worth your while to sacrifice the mints." His gaze lingered wistfully on her lips.

Warmth crept into her cheeks at the prospect of a long, leisurely walk sprinkled with his kisses. What a way to celebrate the first weekend in May. "You think so, do you?"

"I know so. Because—" he leaned in close, his voice lowered to a husky rasp "—I happen to know for a fact which of the three Banks boys...loves you the most."

* * * * *

Don't miss these other HEARTS OF HUNTER RIDGE *stories from Glynna Kaye:*

REKINDLING THE WIDOWER'S HEART
CLAIMING THE SINGLE MOM'S HEART
THE PASTOR'S CHRISTMAS COURTSHIP

Find more great reads at www.LoveInspired.com

Dear Reader,

Is there something in your past that you need to let go of so God can bless your future?

That's a question facing Sawyer and Tori on their rocky road to love. Sawyer is burdened by a guilty conscience, and disappointment from a previous relationship leaves Tori fearful of entering into a new one. Or is the *true* issue standing in the way of finding love in each other's arms the simple fact that they need to grow in their trust of God? That they need to learn to accept by faith that He cares for them and has a good plan for their lives. Just like a little boy who doesn't know he's lost, sometimes we don't recognize that we've wandered far from where we should be until God comes to find us.

I hope you enjoyed returning to the Arizona mountain town of Hunter Ridge as much as I did when writing Sawyer and Tori's journey to a happily-ever-after!

You can contact me via email at glynna@glynna kaye.com or Love Inspired Books, 195 Broadway, 24th Floor, New York, NY 10007. Please visit my website at glynnakaye.com—and stop by loveinspiredauthors.com, seekerville.net, and seekerville.blogspot.com!

Glynna Kaye

THEIR PRETEND AMISH COURTSHIP
The Amish Bachelors • by Patricia Davids

To avoid their matchmaking mothers' plans and pursue their dreams, Fannie Erb and Noah Bowman agree to a pretend courtship. As they make room in their schedules to attend events as a couple, could their hearts also begin to make room for each other?

LONE STAR BACHELOR
The Buchanons • by Linda Goodnight

Content with his bachelor life, builder Sawyer Buchanon's world is turned upside down when he meets pretty PI Jade Warren. Jade was raised to never trust a Buchanon, but when she's hired to investigate the vandalism at Sawyer's building projects, the Texas charmer soon sweeps her off her feet.

SECOND-CHANCE COWBOY
Cowboys of Cedar Ridge • by Carolyne Aarsen

Once she's paid off her father's debts, Tabitha Rennie plans to leave Cedar Ridge and all the painful memories it brings. Having ex-fiancé Morgan Walsh ask for help connecting with his son was not part of the plan. Yet spending time with father and son is creating dreams of house and home.

FALLING FOR THE RANCHER
Aspen Creek Crossroads • by Roxanne Rustand

As a single mom, veterinarian Darcy Leighton would do anything for her daughter—including remaining at the clinic with rancher vet Logan Maxwell, the man who bought the place out from under her. As they work together, their truce turns to friendship—and to the discovery of a once-in-a-lifetime love.

THE SINGLE MOM'S SECOND CHANCE
Goose Harbor • by Jessica Keller

Returning to Goose Harbor, Claire Atwood has plenty of reasons for staying away from Evan Daniels—most notably being jilted at the altar by her onetime sweetheart. But both are running for mayor, which means spending time together. But could it also mean a second chance at forever?

HOMETOWN HERO'S REDEMPTION
by Jill Kemerer

When rugged firefighter Drew Gannon asks her to babysit troubled ten-year-old Wyatt, Lauren Pierce can't help but recall their high school rivalry. Can the temporary single dad prove to the pretty former social worker he's no longer the foolhardy teen she once knew—and he's actually her perfect match?

LICNM0517

Get 2 Free Books,
Plus 2 Free Gifts—
just for trying the Reader Service!

LI17R